Toots

underwater

Toots
underwater

CAROL HUGHES

BLOOMSBURY

First published in Great Britain in 1999
Bloomsbury Publishing Plc, 38 Soho Square, London, W1V 5DF

The moral right of the author has been asserted
A CIP catalogue record of this book is available from the
British Library

ISBN 0 7475 4174 4

Printed in Great Britain by Clays Ltd, St Ives plc

10 9 8 7 6 5 4 3 2 1

For Faith

CHAPTER ONE

~ The River ~

It was summer, a summer to better all summers. The sun was up early each morning and didn't go to bed till late and the sky was blue all day. Toots and her father were spending their holidays, two weeks in all, in a small cottage by the river.

The river was lovely. There were crack willow trees and shady alders along the banks and a forest of tall reeds by the water's edge. Above a small stone dam the river pooled into a shallow reservoir that was perfect for swimming. In a normal year excess water trickled through the sluice in the dam and sparkled merrily as it swirled around the rocks and stones on its way to the sea. But the river was not as full as usual and half the dam stood high and dry. The summer had been long and hot and there had been no rain to replenish the streams. In some places there was hardly any water at all. Below the dam there was a shallow backwater where the weed-covered rocks stood only puddle deep in a bright green, slippery slime.

Along the southern bank of the river there were six cottages with a family staying in each. Toots and her father were staying in number six, the last one in the row. The cottages were separated from each other by the tall trees and when it was quiet outside it was like being alone in the world.

On this particular afternoon, as Toots stared out of the window of her room and listened to the voices of the other children shrill in the summer air, she wished that she *was* all alone in the world, especially after what had happened earlier.

Even though there were hours to go till bedtime and the sun was nowhere near setting, she'd been sent to her room as a punishment and now she wasn't allowed out. She wasn't even allowed any supper and it was all Robbie's fault.

Toots groaned and rolled her eyes. Robbie! He was such a little boy. Such a baby. Robbie and his mother were staying in the cottage next door. Toots's father had made friends with Elaine, Robbie's mother, and now he expected Toots to be best friends with Robbie.

But she couldn't be. For one thing, Robbie was almost a year younger than her and, for another, he couldn't swim. He was afraid of the water and had to wear water wings. He was always asking her to play with him in the shallow stream below the dam where the really little kids played. But Toots didn't want to play there. She wanted to run and scream and splash about in the deeper water with the older children.

Wherever Toots went Robbie tagged along after trying to get her to join in whatever game it was he wanted to play. Robbie's games always seemed to involve rocks or maths or something equally dull. Toots usually stopped listening and hurried towards the river, where she would rush splashing into the deeper water leaving Robbie on the bank. When she looked back, she saw him making his way to the shallows alone.

Robbie spent most of his time paddling in the shallows playing games by himself and looking at the rocks. He knew every one by name and would witter on for hours about them if you let him.

What made it even worse was that Toots's father had invited Robbie and his mother over to supper every single night since they'd arrived. He said it was because their cottage had a picnic table and Elaine and Robbie's did not and besides it was nice to share, but Toots didn't like it.

Her father seemed to think that Robbie's rock stories were the most fascinating he'd ever heard. He was always saying that Robbie was a clever boy. When Toots had tried to get a word in edgeways to tell her father about her day on the river, he'd told her off for being rude and interrupting Robbie, as though he'd actually been interested. After that Toots had made a point of keeping her mouth firmly shut and not saying a word more than was absolutely necessary for the rest of the evening. Nobody had seemed even to notice.

Toots thought about this as she rested her chin on the painted windowsill and watched the topmost branches of the trees wavering against the blue sky. A frown ruffled her brow. It wasn't fair. It seemed as though her father thought that everything Robbie did was rolled in gold while anything she tried was rubbish.

She puckered up her lips, blew out a long sigh and tipped her head to one side so that her cheek lay against the cool windowsill.

Yesterday evening, when her father had come up to say goodnight, he'd kissed her on the forehead and sat on the side of the bed.

'Did you think I was ignoring you at supper?' he'd begun. Toots had shrugged. 'Robbie's a good lad,' he said. Toots pulled a face. She was fed up with hearing how Robbie was a good lad. Her dad tucked the cover under her chin. 'He's had a rough time since his dad left, and his allergies make him feel ill. Besides, he's not got much confidence, that's why it's important to be nice to him. You make friends so easily, sweetheart, I don't think you know how hard it is for Robbie. Try and be kind.'

Toots chewed her lip. She thought that not having

much confidence meant you were shy which meant you didn't say very much and you avoided other people's company. But Robbie wasn't like that. She felt like trying to tell her father that Robbie's problem was that he didn't know how to stop talking, and that he was always going on and on about rocks and trying to join in where he wasn't wanted, but she held her tongue. Her father probably wouldn't be interested. The way he hadn't been interested when she'd tried to tell him that Robbie's stories were boring and he was a pest and that he also had a very annoying habit of breathing loudly through his nose when he ate, which, allergies or not, was revolting.

Toots's father lifted her chin and looked her in the eye. 'You've always had so much confidence, you don't know what it's like not to have any. Try not to tease him or let the others tease him. It's not fair.'

'But Dad, Robbie's so stupid and gullible. He believes anything. Anything.'

'He's not stupid. He's very clever. He certainly knows a lot about geology.' Toots rolled her eyes. 'All right, you may not be interested in it, but I am. What he has to say is quite fascinating if you could be bothered to listen. Now promise me, be nice. Include him in your games with the other children and don't let them tease him the way they do.'

Toots groaned. Her father put on his sternest face

which always made her laugh.

'Toots! Seriously, you will try, won't you?'

And Toots had nodded.

But for all her promises and good intentions the next afternoon had been a complete disaster. It hadn't been her fault. Well, not entirely.

'What about panning for gold in the shallows downstream?' Robbie had piped up in his squeaky little voice when everyone had been deciding what to play that afternoon. "I've got a sieve. It's easy. I can show you what to do.'

'Don't be stupid. There isn't any gold in the river,' Luke had said. Toots had shifted uncomfortably. She'd brought Robbie along and he'd already embarrassed her with his silly suggestions.

Luke was the oldest kid and sort of the leader. He was tough, and if you weren't in his gang you didn't get to play on the rope swing or join in any of the games along the river.

'I think we should play explorers. We'll set up camp over there,' Luke had said, pointing to the small, flat, bramble covered island upstream of the dam. You had to wade waist deep through the river to get there. Robbie had never been that far into the water.

The little group turned as one and squinted at the small, flat, muddy island. Low bushes grew so thick and thorny on the island's narrow beach that it would be impossible to penetrate them without being scratched to ribbons, but Luke was not to be deterred.

'We'll follow this stream,' he continued, 'and climb over the dam and camp there on the haunted island tonight.' Then he had added in a very serious voice, 'You all know it's haunted, don't you? Haunted by the ghosts of people who were eaten by Sally Greenteeth. If you listen very carefully, especially at night, you can hear them moaning. Only the bravest warrior would dare to visit that island at night.'

Even Toots had shivered when she heard this. She'd read about Sally Greenteeth, a water witch who hid in the reeds at night and snatched children off the shore for her supper, and the stories had given Toots nightmares for a week.

Robbie had stood very still and quiet. His face had paled beneath his sunburn and he'd breathed heavily through his nose. Toots could tell he believed every word that Luke had said. She rolled her eyes. Robbie was so gullible. To tell the truth, Toots would have preferred to stay with him on the shore, but she knew that if she did, Luke would make fun of her for being a coward and that would be more than she could bear.

'Hey, Robbie,' said Luke, beckoning him over. Robbie stepped forward a little shyly. 'I think we were wrong about you,' he said looking earnestly at Robbie. 'I think you're really brave and you would quite happily spend a night on the island. You wouldn't be afraid, would you?'

Robbie didn't say anything for a minute, then he shook his head. Luke went on.

'A few of us are going to camp there tonight. We think you should come too!'

Robbie looked over at the island.

'All right,' he said.

Luke was going too far. Toots felt as though she should say something, but she didn't.

'Meet you there at midnight then,' said Luke conspiratorially. The other children stifled giggles behind their hands. 'Come on, last one to the island's a sissy,' Luke had shouted and, kicking up his heels, he led the way, splashing riotously through the water.

Toots didn't want to be left on the shore like Robbie. She got caught up in the revelry and, forgetting her promise to try and be nice and not leave Robbie out, found herself splashing and whooping and hollering along with the others and leaving Robbie very much behind.

'TOOTS!' Her father's call had echoed like thunder across the water. Toots was mortified as her father waded into the water, took her by the arm and dragged her back to the bank in front of everyone. It wasn't fair. The others had left Robbie out too, but she knew without a doubt that she would get all the blame.

Toots knew what was coming. Her father wasn't wearing the stern face that made her laugh now. This was his stern, stern face.

'Toots, you promised,' he'd said in a quiet voice as he'd marched her up the bank past Robbie.

'It wasn't just me. The others . . .' Toots had begun, but the look on her father's face stopped her.

Toots had wriggled and squirmed and twisted her face into a hundred different expressions.

'But he's so stupid and gullible. Now he thinks that Luke and the others want to meet him . . .'

'That's enough!' her father had said, swinging her round. Keeping a firm grip on her shoulder in case she decided to make a break for it, he marched her back to their cottage.

So Toots had been sent to her room while everyone else was still playing outside or eating their suppers or grilling sausages. It wasn't fair, she thought, as she stared out at the trees.

The chink of crockery roused her and she lifted herself up and peered through the window into the garden where her father was setting the picnic table for dinner. He laid out three places on the chequered tablecloth while blue smoke curled into the air from the sausages on the barbecue. Toots was trying not to think about how hungry she was, when Robbie and his mother appeared from beneath the crack willow trees.

Toots turned away and gazed over at the tangle of thorns and brambles on the island in the river. There was something uncomfortable about that place with its muddy, marshy lip of a beach and its prickly thorn bushes.

Robbie's voice drifted up to her window. He was droning on with some long and complicated story which he kept getting wrong and starting all over again. Toots stopped listening and stared at the river.

She hated being stuck in her room. She wished she was a hundred miles from there. She could be, if she ran away. She would have to wait till after dark, but that was no reason why she shouldn't get ready.

She stuffed her pillow under the quilt and pushed it around a bit to make it look as though she was lying there asleep. When she'd finished, it looked just like a pillow stuffed under the bedclothes, but perhaps in the dark it would fool her father. That was if he even bothered to come and say goodnight to her.

She stood up and opened a drawer to get the things she'd need on her journey. The first thing she saw was the velvet ring box.

She picked it up, sat back on the bed and smiled. The box contained her most precious possession, a gold and amethyst ring that her mother had left her. Toots's mother had died a long time ago and this ring was one of the few things that she had to remember her by. It was beautiful. A bright, purple, square-cut stone in a plain gold band. Toots loved to hold it close to her eye and stare deep into the heart of the stone where the light flashed and sparkled.

Her father would not have been pleased if he'd known she'd brought it on holiday with her. He would have said it was too likely to get lost in all the to-ing and fro-ing and the long drive, but Toots had wanted to bring it, so she'd hidden it at the bottom of her bag and had sworn to herself that she would look after it so that nothing would go wrong.

But something did go wrong. Horribly wrong.

She leaned back on the bed and tried to open the box. It was always difficult because the hinge was old and unpredictable. She tried to prise it apart, but she didn't have a good hold on the box and as it opened, it catapulted out of her fingers.

Box and ring parted company. The box clattered to the floor and skidded beneath the bed while the ring shot towards the window. Toots was just quick enough to clap her hands together and catch it between her palms. She lay back on the bed and let out a long breath, then she held the ring in front of her nose and twisted it slowly so that she could watch the lights dance.

She slipped it onto her fattest finger. The ring was slightly too big, which was one of the reasons her father wouldn't let her wear it until she was older. It could easily fall off her finger, but Toots reasoned that she wasn't going to go anywhere wearing it, so it was probably all right.

She jumped to her knees and hung over the edge of the bed to retrieve the box. It had skidded a long way under the bed and as she stretched to reach it, the ring slipped off her finger and rolled away beneath the bed. Toots groaned and slapped her hand on the floor. But she wasn't quick enough this time. The ring rolled into the shadows, fell into a crack between the bare, dusty floorboards and disappeared from sight. In desperation Toots hung further over and ran her hand over the boards, but the ring had gone.

She was just about to jump up and pull the bed out from the wall so that she could search beneath it properly, when she noticed something small glinting like a piece of glitter in the gloom. Toots narrowed her eyes. It was only a tiny glimmer of something stuck in the coarse fabric of the underside of the bed, but there was something very familiar about it. Toots leaned in closer. What was it?

Then suddenly she knew. It was the tiny silver bucket that had been given to her by the garden fairies as a thank you present for when she'd helped them rid the garden of the terrible Waspgnat. She'd put it in her mother's ring box for safe keeping. Toots wondered how she could have forgotten so much.

It is one of the strange things about the Upside Down World that when you leave it and return to your own world you soon forget that the upside down one exists. It was only when Toots stood on her head or leaned over and looked down at the ceiling that she remembered there was such a place at all. Then her memories of the adventures she'd had with Olive and the other fairies rushed back to her, just the way that dreams rush back to you in the middle of the day when you think you've forgotten them entirely. Something small pricks your memory and all at once you can see the whole dream as fresh and as real as if it had just happened.

Toots was staring at the tiny bucket and smiling at her memories when a faint voice interrupted her thoughts.

'Humph!' it said. 'Mumph. Humph. Mumph!'

'Olive?' Toots whispered into the shadows. 'Olive, are you here too?'

CHAPTER TWO

~ The Bocans ~

Toots jumped up, grabbed a flashlight from her drawer and shone it under the bed. A little way away from her tiny silver bucket lay another one tipped over on its side. Beside it was a large, blue-clad bottom and a pair of minute legs waggling in the air.

'Olive!' exclaimed Toots. 'Here, let me help.' She reached out and with the tips of her fingers pulled ever so gently on one of the waggling legs and set Olive the right way up.

Olive was a garden fairy and less than the length of Toots's little fingernail in height. But even though Olive was so much smaller, Toots could see that she was upset from the way that she was jumping up and down.

'Oh dear, oh dear,' Olive puffed in her squeaky little voice. 'What day is it? How long have I been stuck in that box?'

'I'm sorry, Olive,' whispered Toots as quietly as she could so as not to deafen Olive's tiny ears. 'But I can't hear what you're saying.'

Olive reached into the bucket which hung from her belt and pulled out a megaphone. She put it to her lips.

'What day is it?' she asked, her voice booming through the amplifier.

'Wednesday,' replied Toots.

'Oh no, it isn't, is it? Oh no!' Olive let the megaphone fall from her lips, sat down and, burying her tiny face in her tiny hands, began to sob. Toots had never seen her friend so upset. Olive was usually so calm. It upset Toots to see her this way.

'Olive, what's wrong?' she whispered gently. But Olive just kept on sobbing. This went on for almost five minutes. Toots had to do something. She had to take charge. 'Olive,' she said in a firm voice. 'Olive? Listen to me. I want you to dry your eyes and bring me to the Upside Down World. It'll be easier for us to talk then and you can tell me all about it. Is that all right?'

Olive wiped her eyes with the backs of her hands and nodded.

'I'll get under the bed,' said Toots. 'That'll be the safest, easiest way, won't it?'

Olive nodded again.

Toots climbed down and, leaning over, laid the palm of her right hand against the underside of the bed. Olive deftly tied a loop of her cobweb rope around Toots's little finger. Then Toots tried to crawl under the bed, but her head was too large, Not to be defeated, she thought for a moment, then turned around and, lying on her belly like a snake, wriggled back feet first until only her head protruded. She looked like a turtle with the bed the shell on her back.

It was uncomfortable and dusty under the bed. 'The sooner I'm off the floor and down there with Olive the better,' thought Toots with a sniff that turned into a sneeze. 'Ready,' she said.

'Here we go,' cried Olive and she tugged on the rope. Almost immediately Toots began to feel herself getting smaller. First she noticed that the space beneath the bed was larger, and then that by wriggling back she could easily get her head under it. Her gravity still hadn't switched, but she was definitely shrinking. She wriggled further back into the shadows. It was strange easily being able to do something that a moment before she hadn't been able to do at all.

Soon there was room enough for Toots to lift herself on to all fours. She rested the top of her head on the floor, looked down at Olive and watched as the fairy grew bigger and bigger. Toots smiled. It was lovely to see Olive again, even with her tear-stained face.

Apart from the tears Olive was just the way Toots remembered her. Big and round and still dressed in the sparkling, bluebottle-blue uniform of an Upside Down garden fairy cadet. Olive's flying goggles were pushed to the top of her head and her iridescent wings fluttered prettily behind her.

Toots was so busy thinking about how nice it was to see Olive, that she didn't realise how much she'd shrunk and how close she was to having her gravity switch. If she'd been concentrating, she would have remembered that this meant that everything that was up would become down, and everything that was down would become up, but she forgot, and consequently when it happened she was far from ready. She screamed as she fell quickly from the great height of the floor.

It was lucky that the bottom of the bed was soft and springy because the twenty centimetres or so between the floor and the bed was now a great distance. It was like falling from the highest diving board at the swimming pool. Falling backwards from such a height without knowing whether or not you are going to land safely is terrifying. Toots gasped as the air rushed past her. She didn't dare look behind.

'Look out,' hissed Olive.

But Toots couldn't do anything to stop herself or to slow her fall. Suddenly she hit the underside of the bed with a bang. The hessian covering scratched against her legs and hands. But she didn't stay there. The bottom of the bed was as bouncy as a trampoline. Toots shot up in the air again almost all the way to the floor.

'Weeeeee!' she squealed.

'Shush,' warned Olive, trying to catch hold of her hand to stop her from bouncing. 'Be quiet. You never know who might be down here.'

'Goblins?' thought Toots. She had encountered Goblins before. They were horrible. She kept as quiet as she could.

Toots bounced a few more times and with each bounce she shrank a little until she was exactly the size she should have been in the Upside Down World, which was about half as big as Olive.

Eventually she stopped bouncing, got to her knees and tried to stand. But it was like trying to stand on a trampoline. It was too wobbly, so instead she crawled over to Olive and sat down next to her.

'It's lovely to see you again, Olive,' she said. 'But how did you get here and please tell me what's upsetting you so much.'

Olive smiled bravely, but her big chin trembled and it was a moment before she could find her voice.

'I came to your room to look for you,' Olive began. 'And when I found you you were holding that box open in front of your nose. I thought if I stood in it and shouted loud enough you might be able to hear me. So I landed and began to call your name, but I hadn't been there half a minute when you suddenly snapped the box shut trapping me inside and I've been stuck in there ever since. And now you say it's Wednesday.'

Big tears welled up in Olive's eyes and she couldn't go on. She blew her nose on her hanky.

'Oh Olive, what's so terrible about Wednesday?' asked Toots as gently as she could. Olive sniffed back another sob and dabbed at her runny nose.

'It's the day after Tuesday,' she sobbed, making no sense at all. Toots waited patiently while Olive composed herself. 'I was coming to invite you to my graduation. It was to be on Tuesday, which is now yesterday, which means that everything is over. Do you see?' Toots shook her head. Olive tried again. 'I've been taking the entrance examinations to become a river fairy cadet. I only had one more exam to do, the practical river fairy demonstration in the pond, and it's my best subject. The only way I could fail that was not to be there. I was coming to invite you to my graduation after the exam, but now it's too late. I've missed the exam, which means I've failed. I've messed it all up. Now I won't be able to graduate.' Olive began to sob again.

'Olive! Olive!' implored Toots. But Olive kept on crying. Toots felt awful. Olive was usually so full of beans and not at all mopey. Toots was at a loss what to do.

'Can I help?' she asked. Olive shook her head. 'Are you sure?' she asked again. Olive shook her head more ferociously.

'Won't you be able to take the exam again?' asked Toots as gently as she could.

Olive dried her eyes. 'Not for ages,' she said. 'You see the examining board have so many gardens to visit that they only come round once every few years. It's all right,' she sniffed. 'I don't really mind staying in the garden. It's just that . . . well, every garden fairy dreams of being a river fairy. And I really thought that this time I would be able to . . . I would love to have been one.' Olive shook herself and smiled at Toots. 'Well, it was awfully nice of you to come and cheer me up. Perhaps you wouldn't mind coming with me to the garden and helping me explain that I didn't go A.W.O.L.'

Olive stopped suddenly and stared in horror at the floorboards above them.

'Toots,' she gasped. 'This isn't your house, is it? Where are we?' she asked with trembling lips.

'We're on holiday,' said Toots. 'We're staying in this cottage for two weeks.'

Olive's face grew pale. 'How far from home are we?' she asked in a cracking voice.

'It took half a day to drive here. It's by a river and ever so nice.'

'Half a day? Then it's probably too far for me to fly home,' groaned Olive. 'This makes things even worse. I'm going to be in terrible trouble. Now they really will think I've gone A.W.O.L.'

'What's "aywol"?' asked Toots.

'It stands for "absent without leave",' answered Olive. 'Cadets aren't allowed to do it. I could be court martialled if my Group Captain thinks that I've run away. I must get going and report to the nearest Upside Down Squadron immediately. If we're lucky, they'll have a field telephone and I'll be able to ring home.'

When Olive said 'ring', Toots remembered her amethyst ring and how she still had to retrieve it from the hole in the floor.

'Olive, wait,' she said. Toots quickly explained all about her ring. Olive listened carefully and by the time Toots had finished speaking, she had come up with a plan.

'If you wait here, I'll fly up to the floor and see if I can see it through the crack in the floorboards. If I can reach it, I'll tie one end of my rope to it then, when you're big again and before your memory of the Upside Down World fades, you can pull it out of the hole.'

This seemed like a fine plan. Olive was looping the cobweb rope into a coil when suddenly she shivered.

'There's something odd about this place,' she said as she peered into the shadows.

Toots nodded. She's noticed it at the same moment. She looked around and stared at the farthest reaches of the floor above them. A thin rim of gold glinted in the darkest, dustiest corner.

'That's my ring,' she whispered urgently. Then her eyes opened wide. How had it come out of the hole and why did it appear to be moving towards them? Toots blinked.

'Olive?' she began.

'Shush!' warned Olive. She sniffed, then threw her hand over her mouth to stifle a cough. Toots had noticed the terrible smell too and was about to ask what it could be when Olive let out a little scream.

'Oh,' she gasped.

Suddenly Olive grabbed Toots's wrist and hoisted her to her feet.

'What is it?' Toots asked in a terrified voice.

'Quick!' Olive whispered. 'No time to explain. Hurry, pick up your bucket and let's go!'

With great difficulty they set off towards the front edge of the bed, sinking up to their knees in the springy fabric with every step. It was like trying to run across very firm but bouncy jelly.

Olive roughly pulled Toots towards the bed leg, which stood as tall as a church tower in the far corner. Toots could hardly keep her balance and more than once she stumbled and fell. Each time Olive had to turn back and pull her up again.

Finally they reached the shelter of the bed leg and Olive ducked behind it, yanking Toots after her.

'Goblins?' asked Toots in a low whisper as she peered around the bed leg. Olive shook her head.

'Worse! Much worse,' she hissed under her breath. 'Only the Bocans smell as bad as that!' Toots didn't know exactly what Olive meant by the Bocans, but she knew she didn't want to meet them.

'Couldn't we just fly away?' she whispered, looking around desperately. 'What about the Upside Down House in this cottage? Couldn't we just fly there?'

'No time. The Bocans'll spot us for sure if we do and the chances are they'll shoot us down easy as anything. Don't be afraid. If we stay hidden they may pass us by.'

Toots felt a little unnerved by this. Olive had only said that they 'might' pass by. Toots swallowed, then kept very still and watched as the ring passed out of the darkest shadows and into the gloomy half light under the bed. Her heart beat faster as she stared up at the floor. The ring moved closer and the awful smell got stronger. Then she saw the Bocans approaching through the gloom. They were truly terrifying.

Two horrible creatures, far more revolting than anything Toots had ever seen before, were struggling to carry her amethyst ring across the floor. A third walked behind them twisting his head from side to side and glaring ferociously in every direction.

The Bocans, like their foul cousins the goblins, live the same way up as humans, which meant that they were now upside down to Toots. But even seeing them upside down was unnerving enough.

Toots covered her nose with the hem of her T-shirt to stop herself from coughing, but she couldn't entirely block out the foul stench. Her eyes watered, it was so pungent.

The three Bocans smelled of all the horrible smells in all the world mixed together. They smelled of old sour dishcloths which had been screwed up and left to rot in the corner of the kitchen on a hot summer's day. They smelled of rotten eggs, of dirty nappies, of rancid fat. They smelled of the water at the bottom of flower vases when all the flowers have died. But however bad the three Bocans smelled it wasn't half as horrible as they way they looked.

Toots began to shake as they drew nearer. Olive set a steady hand on her shoulder and gave her a warning glance.

The Bocans' bodies were ingrained with dirt. They were as pink as pigs in places, but dark as pitch in the folds and wrinkles of their skin where the dirt had gathered. Their hide was slimy and sparsely covered in short wiry hairs that were plastered flat with grease. Their bellies were big and round, and dimpled with craterous pockmarks, and their shoulders were hunched high above their heads, which made them look like toads. Their broad fingernails were yellow and cracked and black rimmed, as though they had spent their lives digging through hardened muck with their callused hands.

The Bocans' eyes were so narrow and piercing that they could have bored a hole in a slab of steel and the baggy wrinkles around them were as red and as raw as old bacon and hung halfway down their cheeks like festoons of raffia. Their noses were large and flabby and a thick bush of stiff black hair stuck out of each gaping nostril. Their mouths were wide and loose and when opened, revealed small, brick-like teeth that were stubby and caked in a stinking green moss. Their arms and legs, where exposed, were podgy and covered in warts and knobbly scars, some of which were fresh and bloody. Two of the Bocans had deep old scars across their faces, but the third's head was covered by a helmet which ended at his nose. There were two narrow slits in the metal through which his piercing eyes shone. His slobbering lips protruding below the helmet were covered in boils and warts.

But revolting and filthy and smelly as the Bocans were, their armour was immaculate. They all wore highly polished, leather breastplates. The leather was as shiny as a conker and was fastened over their shoulders with gleaming brass rings. These breastplates were inlaid with finely worked silver shields and dotted with bright studs.

The weapons they carried were well polished too. The smallest Bocan carried a silver bow, and a quiver full of arrows hung from a loop on his belt. The one with the helmet wore a short broadsword in an ornate scabbard decorated with silver spirals. The third carried a silver tipped spear with jewels set into the shaft.

The two Bocans struggled and grumbled as they carried the ring. They wheezed and huffed and sounded like old traction engines scraping over rusty tracks.

Toots looked at Olive and saw that she had grown very pale and her big cheeks were trembling in fear. When Toots saw that, she became frightened. She knew that Olive was not easily intimidated, so if she was scared, there was probably something to be scared about.

Toots stared up at her amethyst ring. Bocans or no Bocans she had to get it back somehow, but she knew it wasn't going to be easy. The Bocans didn't look like the types who would kindly hand something back once you'd explained that it didn't belong to them. They looked more like the types who would string you up by your ankles and roast you slowly over a blazing fire if you so much as dared to breathe in their presence. But even so Toots knew she had to do something.

'Olive?' she hissed as quietly as she could. Olive winced and put her finger to her lips, warning Toots to be silent. But it was too late. The Bocans had heard something. The ring clattered to the floor as they dropped it and reached for their weapons.

'Fairies?' growled the one in the helmet, drawing his sword and holding it high in front of him.

'More of them?' asked the smallest one, drawing out one of the long arrows and setting it in his bow.

'No,' croaked the one with the spear. 'We got all of them. Every one. None left now. That was just the trees creaking in the wind. Listen.'

The Bocans stood as still as stones, poised and dangerous. Olive and Toots barely dared to breathe. Toots could hear her heart thumping hard against her chest. She only hoped that the Bocans couldn't hear it too.

They couldn't. Outside, the wind blew through the trees and the Bocans relaxed.

'See!' said the one with the spear.

Cautiously, they put their weapons away and squatted down beside the ring. They cleared their throats and spat on the dusty floor. Light bounced off the gold and lit up their horrible faces.

'His Terribleness'll like this,' said the one in the helmet, sniffing the gold ring with his horrible nostrils flaring. 'Very pretty he'll look.'

'Almost as pretty as you, Loach, in that thing you call an helmet,' snorted the littlest Bocan. 'Couldn't you have got a better one? What do you think, Sedge?'

'Shut it, Bog Bean,' growled Loach, grabbing Bog

Bean by the throat and drawing him close. The littlest Bocan struggled fiercely, but Loach, his thick warty lips glossy with slobber, grinned because Bog Bean couldn't reach his weapons. Loach pushed him away and sneered. 'Nobody asked your opinion on nothing. Besides, soon as we've sold this beauty, I'll buy myself a proper helmet. Something beautiful in silver.'

'If you earn enough from carrying *my* gold.' said Sedge with quiet menace. 'Now move it!'

Above them, Toots and Olive watched as Loach tried to lift the heavy ring. It was beyond him. He gave up and flumped back down to the floor.

'It wouldn't be so hard if some people would lend us a hand,' he said sarcastically.

'Shut it,' warned Sedge. 'Pick it up and get moving.'

'It's too heavy,' said Loach, not stirring. 'We can't carry it all the way back to camp, can we?'

Bog Bean cleared his horrible narrow throat. 'Why don't we . . . well, I mean what if . . . I mean . . .' He began to trot excitedly about in a strange, simpering, little dance.

'What? What if we what?' Through the slits in his helmet Loach's eyes blazed with irritation and even more drool dribbled from his lips and made a sticky pool on the floor.

'Well I thought that perhaps . . .' Bog Bean's tittering high voice fluttered in the air.

'Get on with it!' growled Loach.

Bog Bean dropped his head down and mumbled into his chest, 'We could roll it, then it wouldn't be so hard.'

Loach laughed and raised his fist. Bog Bean changed instantly. In a flash he brought his bow up, snatched an arrow from his quiver, set it in place and pointed it at Loach's belly.

'Stop it!' roared Sedge. 'Put that away. You,' he pointed a fat finger at Loach. 'Do what he says. Lift that ring on its side and start rolling. The sooner we get going, the sooner we can get that metal melted down and that stone chipped into fragments for new arrowheads. And the sooner we do that, the sooner we'll have our money. Now come on!' Sedge started towards the door.

The two remaining Bocans set their greasy fingers on the gold ring and with a great deal of humphing finally succeeded in lifting it onto its edge. Then they rolled it towards the door. Bog Bean's idea had been a good one. The ring rolled so fast that they had to hurry to keep up with it. They hit it with their swords to make sure that it stayed upright and in this way rolled the ring right under the bedroom door and disappeared from sight. Toots and Olive stayed still until the 'clang clang clang' of the swords against the gold had faded into the distance.

When all was silent Olive and Toots cautiously

emerged from their hiding place. Toots stared after the Bocans.

'Olive,' she said, outraged and upset. 'They're going to melt my ring down and make swords from it. They are going to chip the lovely amethyst into fragments to make arrowheads.' Her cheeks flushed red with anger. 'Olive, we've got to do something. You have to help me. We have to get it back.'

Olive said nothing. Toots turned and found that Olive was no longer beside her. She had moved away and was standing by the very edge of the bed peering down at the ceiling.

'Toots, come here and look,' called Olive. Toots walked over the springy fabric to join her.

'What is it?' she asked. 'What's wrong?'

Olive turned big frightened eyes towards Toots. 'Look!' She pointed down towards the ceiling.

'What?' asked Toots staring over the edge of the bed. The ceiling was cracked in places, but more or less bare. 'I don't see anything.'

'Exactly!' said Olive. Toots looked puzzled. 'I don't like it. The Bocans said the fairies had gone. That they'd got every one of them.' Toots nodded. She was beginning to understand. Olive went on. 'Oh Toots, what did they mean? We have to find out what's happened. Come on. I promise I'll help you rescue your ring later, but right now we've got to get to the Upside

Down House. Quick, run as best you can and I'll fly behind you and pick you up.'

Toots remembered how this went. Olive wasn't strong enough to take off with Toots from a standing start. She needed some added momentum.

Toots started to run across the springy hessian. The faster she went, the easier it was. She ran towards the shadows then turned and rushed towards the edge of the bed. If Olive didn't lift her up before she reached it, she was in danger of overshooting and falling all the way to the ceiling which for someone who was less then a centimetre tall was a very long way. Thankfully she soon heard the burr of Olive's wings behind her and just as she reached the edge Olive grabbed her by the waist and lifted her up. Toots gasped as they flew over the edge of the bed and the now enormous cottage bedroom opened up beneath them.

CHAPTER THREE

~ Another Upside Down House ~

Olive beat her wings and flew towards the ceiling.
'Who are the Bocans?' asked Toots as they flew.

'They are the worst of the goblin families,' replied Olive. 'War-mongering scoundrels. Horrible creatures. They are usually too busy fighting each other over gold to bother with us, but if they are here then they have been brought here for some purpose. They are mercenary to the last and, even though they enjoy fighting more than anything, they only attack non-Bocans if there's money in it.'

'Who would have brought them here?'

'Somebody who was up to no good,' Olive replied as she flew in low over the ceiling.

Toots, remembering how to land without falling over, began to circle her legs and run in the air. Olive flew lower and Toots's feet connected smoothly with the ceiling. Then, as Olive let go, she kept on running until she was steady enough to slow down. Olive landed beside her and, without losing any time, began to search for signs of fairy life.

'This doesn't look right,' she muttered in a very worried tone. 'There are no new cobwebs for one thing and these footprints are old.'

Toots looked at the mess of fairy cadet footprints on the ceiling. Olive was right. They were pale and chalky in the dusky light and far from fresh. The cobwebs in the corners of the room were broken and the pretty lights that normally sparkled along their strands when you looked at them up close were dull and faded.

'It's been a long time since I was a house fairy cadet,' said Olive sadly. 'But I remember one thing. No fairy would let this happen in her house. It's awful.'

As Toots followed Olive across the ceiling, she suddenly had the uneasy feeling that someone was watching her from behind. She turned round. There was nothing there except the blank ceiling stretching off into the distance behind her. But she couldn't shake the feeling. She looked up at the vast room above her. The cottage bedroom was full of nooks and crannies and if someone was watching her, they could have been hiding anywhere. Toots shuddered and hurried after Olive.

There was a small door in the corner of the ceiling. Olive gently pushed on it, and it swung open with an eerie creak. Toots followed.

Beyond the door there was a short flight of five steps leading down on to a long corridor. Everything looked just as it should in any Upside Down House. The lights burned in dainty chandeliers, the floor was covered with a bright carpet, the doors were painted pretty colours and there were pictures in frames hanging on the walls. But everything did not *feel* just as it should. There was no sound from anywhere.

The emptiness in the corridor felt peculiar. In a normal Upside Down House the corridors rarely stayed empty for long. There was usually somebody hurrying here or there, and even if they were empty they were never this quiet. The sounds of fairies busy at their work or their lessons could usually be heard as a low murmur in the background. Here there was nothing but silence.

The treads of the stairs creaked as Toots and Olive made their way down. Toots held her bucket close so that it did not rattle; its rattling jarred her nerves and the eerie silence was making her nervous enough as it was.

'Where is everybody?' whispered Olive when they reached the foot of the stairs. 'Surely an entire squadron can't just have disappeared.'

Toots felt again that she was being watched. It was a creepy feeling. Down the corridor the doors stood open. Toots couldn't be certain, but she thought she saw a shadow flit behind one of them.

Olive pushed the first classroom door. They peered in as it creaked open. The room was a mess. It looked as though a brawl had taken place. Tables and chairs had been tipped over on to the floor and torn papers were flung about. It had been ransacked. And there were arrows stuck into the walls and floors.

'The Bocans!' hissed Olive, pointing at the muddy, splayed footprints covering the ceiling. 'But why would someone pay the Bocans to attack an Upside Down House?'

Olive hurried down the corridor opening doors. It was the same story in every room. Behind the last door they found the cadet's dining hall. The food was still on the table. The fairies must have been attacked while they were having their tea.

Olive touched the teapot. 'Stone cold,' she said, glancing at the congealed food on the plates and then around the room. She pulled one of the many Bocan arrows from the wall and studied its tip, then, turning a chair the right way up, she sat down and shook her head.

'What would the Bocans want with house fairies?' she asked in a mystified voice.

Toots looked around the room. It was in a dreadful state. Most of the cupboard doors were hanging off their hinges and what was once inside the cupboards was now outside and strewn all over the floor. Chairs were overturned and the pictures on the walls hung crooked. Once so nice and neat, everything now lay in ruins.

She had never seen anything like it. Not even her own bedroom had ever been as messy as this. Carefully she stepped over the debris, made her way to the window and stared at the world outside in its strange upside down position. The tree tops reached down towards the sky. Toots tipped her head to one side so that she didn't feel so far away from home. She could hear the children from the other cottages laughing somewhere up amongst the feet of the trees. She could also hear her father and Elaine and Robbie talking over supper and she wrinkled her nose and shook her head.

Again she had the feeling that someone was watching her. She straightened herself and turned her head a little to the right and as she did, a strange thing happened. She saw or thought she saw a blurred fluttering at the outside corner of her right eye, as though something was happening on the farthest edge of her vision. Something she couldn't quite see. It was startling and strange, but didn't last very long because as Toots swung round, it suddenly stopped.

Toots looked at Olive to see if she had noticed anything unusual, but Olive was still studying the arrow and was lost in thought. Toots didn't want to disturb her.

Perhaps it was nothing, she thought, rubbing her eyes. Perhaps it was just an eyelash. She turned her attention back to the window and blinked as she noticed that the branch outside was covered in a wide trail of fairy bootprints stretching all the way to the trunk of the tree.

'Olive, look!' she said. 'Maybe the fairies escaped this way.' Olive got up quickly and joined Toots at the window.

'That wasn't the way they escaped,' said a small voice behind them. 'That was the way they were taken!'

CHAPTER FOUR

~ Rebecca Watts, House Fairy ~

After nearly jumping out of their skins Olive and Toots spun around to see a short, stocky fairy with a shock of wiry black hair and a white, white face climbing out of a cupboard. The fairy smiled at them shyly. Her uniform was filthy and covered in dust. The fairy seemed embarrassed by her appearance and tried to smooth out the front of her jacket and her pink tutu as much as she could, but they were very crumpled and creased. Her hands and face were dirty too.

'What happened here?' asked Olive. 'Where's your C.O.? Where are all the other cadets?'

The fairy stood to attention, saluted and said in the clipped voice of one delivering information to a superior, 'The C.O., other officers and all cadets have all been captured by the Bocans. Cadet Rebecca Watts reporting.'

'It's all right,' said Olive gently. 'You don't have to salute me. I'm not an officer. But even so I'd like to know what happened.'

Rebecca Watts looked miserable.

'It was awful,' she began with a sniff. 'We were just about to start our tea when suddenly they were here, the Bocans, and so many of them that there was little we could do. There was all sorts of fighting and fairies rushing about like mad and someone shoved me out of the way and pushed me into this cupboard. I must have banged my head on the way in or fainted, because I wouldn't have just stayed in there. When I came to, it was all quiet. I peeked out and saw the fairies all chained together being led off along the tree branch.'

'Where did the Bocans take them?'

'I don't know,' she wailed. 'I would have tried to find them, but I couldn't desert my post and even if I had, I wouldn't have been able to get very far. I'm only a house fairy and I can't fly. Ohhhh, I wish I'd been taken along as well.'

Great heaving sobs shook the short fairy's shoulders. Olive wrapped a comforting arm around her and guided her to a chair. Toots hung back by the window and eyed the fairy in the tattered outfit with suspicion. There was something that deeply bothered her about Cadet Rebecca Watts, but she couldn't put her finger on what it was.

'Don't cry,' said Olive. 'You did very well to stay here and guard the house on your own.' But Rebecca only cried harder.

Toots wrinkled her nose. What was it that was bothering her? Was it the way Rebecca Watts was crying? She looked like someone who was only pretending to cry, covering their face and making boo hoo hoo noises, while all the time peeking out between their fingers to make sure everyone had noticed. Toots shook herself. Perhaps she was just being silly. If there was something wrong about Rebecca, Olive would have noticed it too, wouldn't she?

Rebecca lifted her head and blinked at Toots. Her innocent eyes were red rimmed and her cheeks were wet. This cleared Toots's doubts about the tears being real or not, but the queer suspicion lingered.

Olive handed Rebecca a handkerchief. 'Do you know what the Bocans are doing here?' she asked while Rebecca wiped her eyes.

Rebecca shook her head and bit her lower lip.

'Not to worry,' said Olive, 'though I'd like to know who brought them here. A river is not their normal habitat. They don't much care for water and aren't often found by it at all. Someone must be paying them well to be here. I'd like to know who.' Olive paused and tapped her finger against her lips. 'Rebecca?' she asked after a moment. 'I hate to mention this, but has there been anything strange on the river besides the Bocans? Any marsh imps, for example?'

Rebecca's eyes opened wide. 'No,' she said emphatically. 'We've never had marsh imps on our river. Never!' Then she dropped her face in her hands once more and her shoulders shook with sobs.

Olive stood up. 'I'm going to go and check on the Upside Down Houses in the other cottages. See what they know about this. Perhaps I'll find someone who can help.' She nodded at Toots. 'You stay here and look after Rebecca. I'll be back as soon as I can.'

Toots wasn't very happy about being left with Rebecca, but before she could protest, Olive had flown out of the window and was soaring up towards the ground. Toots stared after Olive wishing that she'd taken her along as well.

CHAPTER FIVE

~ The Naiad ~

Rebecca sat down beside Toots and Toots shifted uncomfortably in her seat.

'What kind of fairy are you?' asked Rebecca politely.

'I'm not a fairy,' replied Toots. 'I'm a girl. A house child.'

'No? Really?' Rebecca leaned away from Toots to get a better look at her. 'I've always wanted to meet one of you.' And she smiled a bright, wide, charming smile. 'It must be so wonderful to be a house child. You hear such fabulous stories about them. How clever they are.' Rebecca's eyes shone and she looked so sweet that Toots began to feel that perhaps she was wrong to be suspicious of Rebecca.

'Yes,' said Rebecca, 'everyone always says how clever house children are.' Then a faraway look came into her eyes and she stared past Toots to the window. 'But all the cleverness in the world isn't going to help us here. Not now there's a Naiad in the river,' she whispered softly.

Toots's ears pricked up. 'What's a Naiad?' she asked.

'Oh,' said Rebecca looking shocked. 'I'm sorry. I didn't

realise I said that out loud. It's nothing. Nothing at all.'

'Please tell me,' said Toots gently. 'What's a Naiad – that was what you called it, wasn't it? I'd like to help if I can.' Rebecca shook her head. Toots tried again. 'It wouldn't hurt just to tell me about it, would it?'

Rebecca glanced nervously out of the window, then clasped Toots's hand. Suddenly the little fairy seemed so much older. Her voice sank to a low, urgent whisper.

'All right,' she began. 'But I'm telling you this in the strictest, strictest secrecy. No one must know that I've told you. Please promise you won't tell anyone what I'm going to tell you? And you won't give me away?'

'I promise.' Toots nodded eagerly. She was itching to know what Rebecca was going to say.

'I mean it, no one,' Rebecca said sternly. 'Not even your friend the garden fairy.'

'Olive?' Toots hesitated. 'But Olive wouldn't tell anyone.'

'No,' urged Rebecca. 'Not even her. Promise. You must promise.'

'All right,' she laughed and wondered why Rebecca was being so dramatic. Toots crossed her finger over her heart. 'I won't breathe a word to anyone. Not even Olive. I promise.'

'Good.' Rebecca paused. She took a deep breath. 'I'm not an ordinary house fairy cadet,' she, said, giving Toots a knowing look.

Toots narrowed her eyes. She had known there was something different about Rebecca. She'd know it from the first.

'I think,' said Rebecca with a wry smile, 'that you were clever enough to spot that right away, weren't you? I could tell that you thought my tears seemed a little false by the way you were looking at me, but I had to put on that act for reasons I'll explain to you in a minute.'

'As to not being an ordinary house fairy,' continued Rebecca dropping her voice even lower. 'I'm with the Special Forces. I'm working undercover because there's a terrible problem on the river.' Rebecca narrowed her eyes and glanced out of the window again. She cleared her throat. 'A Naiad has invaded the river. It's an ancient water sprite that comes to poison not only the water in which it lives, but also the land around it. It must be destroyed. If it isn't, all the fairies and the creatures in the river and on the riverbanks soon will be. Look at the island: already nothing grows there but thorns and brambles.

Toots nodded. She'd always thought there was something wrong with that place. Rebecca turned sorrowfully towards the window and seemed unable to continue for a moment.

'The Naiad that infests our river is the worst of all. It brought the Bocans here. The house fairies knew about this and brought us in to do something, but before we had the chance the Bocans attacked and captured all the house fairies and imprisoned them by the dam. The Naiad is a cunning, evil thing and it has already destroyed my home.' Rebecca thumped her fist into her palm. A faint, rust-coloured bruise appeared. She hastily rubbed her hand and the bruise vanished.

'Why didn't you tell all this to Olive?' asked Toots. 'She would have understood.'

Rebecca shook her head. 'I couldn't risk it. To tell a strange fairy could put my entire squadron and all the house fairies in danger. How was I to know that she was who she said she was? How was I to know she wasn't a marsh imp disguised as a house fairy?' Rebecca turned sharply to Toots. 'What do you know about marsh imps?' she demanded.

'Nothing,' replied Toots.

Rebecca shuddered. 'Marsh imps are horrible. They can come to you in any form. They are shape shifters.' She shuddered again. 'I was suspicious when your friend mentioned them. It's a cunning ploy that the imps sometimes use to convince you that they are who they're pretending to be. If they talk about imps as the enemy, suddenly you trust them much more. Do you see?' Toots nodded. 'That's why I was suspicious of your friend the garden fairy.'

'Oh no,' protested Toots. 'Olive's definitely Olive.

You can take my word for that. Besides, how do you know I'm not one of these shape shifter things pretending to be a house child?'

Rebecca smiled. 'Good question. You *are* clever, aren't you? I know you're what you say you are because humans are very difficult for shape shifters to imitate. Something of the imp always remains visible. But you're clever to be cautious. No one can be trusted, no one.'

She was silent for a moment. Her eyes flickered towards Toots and then away again. She swallowed as if her throat was too tight. Then she squeezed Toots's hand harder.

'But I'm going to have to trust you,' she hissed in a strained, urgent voice. 'Will you help us, Toots? We have to fight this terrible thing. Remember this has to be top secret.'

Toots nodded. 'What do you want me to do?'

'Just keep your eyes and ears open and we'll be in touch. The password is "Pike"; the response must be "Eel". Use it so that you always know who you're speaking to and can't be fooled by any impostors. And remember, not a word to anyone.'

'How will I find you?'

'Don't worry. We'll find you!' Rebecca's eyes flickered to the window. 'Get down!' she hissed, suddenly pushing Toots to the floor. 'Bocan soldiers!'

Toots cowered by the bench of the window seat and

saw five Bocan soldiers of assorted shapes and sizes marching along the bottom of the highest branch.

Toots desperately tried to think of something to do to make the Bocans go away. Rebecca kneeled beside her and peeked over the seat.

Out of the very far corner of her eye, Toots glimpsed something flickering. It was a flutter of red as though someone was waving a red handkerchief just out of her sight. She lifted her head quickly. Rebecca was still crouching by the window. She hadn't moved at all.

'They've turned back,' she said.

Toots looked past her and saw that she was right. The Bocans were waddling towards the tree trunk. Rebecca let out a sigh of relief.

'You're very brave, Toots,' she said giving Toots's arm a squeeze. 'I'm glad you're with us. Only the bravest are ever invited to help us.'

Toots forgot about the strange flickering movement she'd seen and swelled with pride. It made her happy that Rebecca thought she was so much braver than she actually was. She didn't bother to tell her how scared she'd been.

Just then Olive flew back in through the window. The news from the other cottages wasn't good.

'It's terrible,' she said as she landed noisily on the messy floor. 'All the Upside Down Houses are deserted. All the house fairies have gone and all of their things have been ransacked.'

'What shall we do?' asked Toots.

Olive shook out her wings. 'Get away from here for a start, it's crawling with Bocans out there. Then we need to see if we can find the house fairies. The Bocans must have them hidden somewhere.'

Toots opened her mouth and was about to say how the Bocans had all the house fairies imprisoned by the dam when Rebecca gave her a warning look. Toots realised that if she told Olive even the smallest detail of what Rebecca had told her, Olive would wonder how she knew and would want to know everything. Toots would have told Olive everything quite happily, but remembering her promise to Rebecca she kept quiet.

'I'll have to carry you both,' Olive continued. 'It'll be slower, but one under each arm will be the best way. If we climb out of the window we can take off from that branch.'

Rebecca paled. 'Oh . . . no . . . I can't come,' she said. 'I have to stay here. I can't fly. I mean, I can't have you fly for me. I mean, I'm not supposed to fly before I have my own set of wings, am I?' Rebecca looked relieved as though she had thought of this rule just in time.

Olive gave her a long look. 'No, you're right, officially you're not, but we could call this an evacuation, couldn't we?'

'I'd rather just stay here if it's all the same to you.'

Rebecca was squirming now. 'I'd feel as though I was deserting my post if I left.'

'All right then,' nodded Olive. 'We'll be back as soon as we can. Come on, Toots.'

'Will you be all right here on your own?' Toots asked Rebecca.

Rebecca nodded. 'I think so,' she replied. 'Good luck!'

Toots nodded secretly at Rebecca and then climbed out of the window and onto the branch.

CHAPTER SIX

~ The Bocan Camp ~

Toots crept a little way along the branch. It wasn't all that wide and it was rather bumpy. The idea of running along it made her feel queasy. But Toots knew that if she was to get to the bottom of this strange mystery and save the river she would have to do it.

She looked back at Olive and waited for her signal.

'Run!' mouthed Olive silently.

Toots took a deep breath and ran as best she could along the uneven surface. She had only gone five or six paces when Olive flew up behind her and carried her away. Toots closed her eyes.

When she dared to open them Olive was swooping down towards the sky. Toots clung tightly to Olive's sleeves. The sky spread out beneath her, a beautiful pale blue ocean of air. Toots gasped. She had forgotten how wonderful it was to fly outdoors.

Above them the river shone silver and gold in the pretty evening light. The cottages were honey coloured and their windows were on fire. Toots could see the other children splashing into the water from the swing. A small figure wandered alone on the river bank close to the island.

'Robbie,' she thought with a little stab of irritation. What was he up to? He disappeared from sight as Olive flew down past the tree tops.

They went down for what felt like a kilometre or more, aiming straight for the sky. Toots's ears burned with the wind and the skin on her face smarted. But she hardly noticed. Her mind was full of secrets and the daunting task that lay ahead. She felt special to have been chosen to be one of a select team. She only wished that she could tell Olive about it, but she couldn't break her promise.

Eventually Olive slowed down and, banking steeply to the right, turned up towards the ground once more and hovered. The river glittered far above them.

'We should be well out of their range up here,' she said, fishing in her bucket and pulling out a small pair of field glasses. Toots clung to the one arm Olive still had around her. She always felt dreadfully uncomfortable when Olive let go with one hand while they were flying and she wished she wouldn't do it so casually.

Olive peered up at the river through the glasses. 'Hmmmm,' she said. 'Hmmmmmmm.'

She handed the powerful glasses to Toots. 'See

there, by the dam,' she said. 'In the reeds, above that thick cloud of midges, that's where the Bocans' camp will be.' Olive began to fly towards it. 'I had to read up on the Bocans for my exams. Rotten lot they are.'

'Olive, wait,' said Toots, whose head was full of dramatic imaginings. She was trying to think what she would be called on to do by the Upside Down Special Forces.

Olive tightened her hold on Toots's middle and with a flutter of her wings began to fly up towards the river. 'Let's have a look and see what's going on up there,' she said. 'The Bocans won't be expecting anyone to approach from this angle and if we're very careful, I dare say we could have a look around – see if we can find your ring. Keep quiet though. Not a word.'

Olive flew up to the river slowly and quietly. Below the layer of buzzing midges was a thick bank of black smoke that came from the Bocans' fires and settled like a fog above their camp. The Bocans lit fires even on the warmest days because they always felt cold and damp, especially when they were near water, which they didn't much like.

Olive flew into the forest of reeds downwind of the Bocans' camp, so that the Bocans wouldn't be able to smell them coming.

Unfortunately they could smell the Bocans. Even when masked by the smoke, the Bocan smell was unmistakably foul.

Olive hovered by the bottom of a reed close to the muddy ground and helped Toots to climb on to it. Then she climbed on to the one beside it.

Toots and Olive stared at the Bocan camp through the smoke.

It was a horrible sight. The Bocans were everywhere. Toots shuddered. If they were discovered hiding in the reeds, she didn't know if they'd be able to escape.

The evening sunlight couldn't penetrate the heavy black mist and the camp was dark and gloomy. Smoking torches burned in tall brackets throwing flickering shadows across the muddy ground.

Toots shook with fear and her reed wavered. Bocans were trampling back and forth through the mud with a sinister squelching sound. There were old Bocans who wore gold armour and carried ornate weapons and young Bocans whose plain leather armour was strapped together with neatly plaited twine. There were female Bocans who wore their hair long and braided and looped up into their helmets and whose armour was not ornamented with gold or silver. And there were two Bocan children running around wielding child-sized swords and swinging at each other viciously until their mothers gave them both a clonk on the head and told them if they were going to fight they should do it properly and not mess around.

There were five large tents in the camp. Four of them were made from thick, brown leaves draped over a circular wicker frame and held in place with ropes made from twisted reeds. Smoke poured through the hole at the top of the tents and hung in swathes around the entrances where the leaf curtains had been peeled back. A burning torch was set at the entrance to each. Inside, the tents were dark and full of shadows.

The fifth tent was different. It was larger than the rest and it wasn't wrapped in leaves. It was draped in something that looked like a scrap of tea towel which might once have been red and white, but was now so scorched and dirty that it was difficult to tell. Beside the entrance a filthy pennant hung limply on a pole and two torches burned instead of just one.

Olive pulled out her field glasses and peered at the pennant trying to make it out.

'Oh,' she groaned. 'No!'

'What?' whispered Toots.

'If I remember correctly,' answered Olive, 'that pennant belongs to Bladderwort the Vain and Terrible, the bloodiest of all the Bocans.' Olive bit her lip, 'Just pray the house fairies got away somehow.'

In the middle of the camp was a great pile, almost a mountain, of what Toots at first thought was rubbish. Then, as her eyes grew accustomed to the light, she realised it was the Bocans' hoard. There were beads and gold paper wrappings from sweets. There were fragments of broken glass and broken links of silver chain. There were even tiny bits of eggshell and screwed up balls of coloured cellophane. But there was no sign of Toots's amethyst ring.

Beside the pile a fire glowed with white hot coals in a huge brazier and next to this the Bocan weapons-smith, a gross bloated Bocan with a great scar running down the side of his face, picked a red-hot sword blade out of the fire with his tongs and immersed it in the bucket of water at his side. The hiss of steam sounded like a pig screaming. Toots blocked her ears. The Bocan smith set the blade on his anvil and began to hammer it flat. The sound rang sharp and discordant across the camp. Around him his assistants fetched and carried all he needed, while others sat bent over little stumpy tables fashioning the melted metal into jewelled axe heads or fancy brooches.

'They're like magpies,' whispered Toots in a very quiet voice. 'They collect shiny things, don't they? I wonder if they get as angry as magpies if you try and take their things away? Magpies go insane.' Toots stopped. She realised that Olive wasn't listening and she felt a little annoyed. Not with Olive but with herself because she realised that she was repeating something that Robbie had told her.

'Shush.' Olive touched Toots's arm. 'Let's go,' she mouthed. Toots was about to follow when the three Bocans they had seen at the house came into the camp rolling her ring in front of them. Toots squeaked when she saw them and squeaked again as they leaned it up against the pile by the fire. The Bocan smith stopped hammering and began to examine it.

Olive quickly clamped her hand over Toots's mouth to stop her squeaking a third time as the Bocan smith, after a brief discussion with the three Bocans, rolled her ring over to the great fire and let it drop. A million bright orange sparks flew up from the embers and vanished into the dark smoke. The flames roared around the ring. Only the amethyst stuck out clear of the fire. The Bocan smith gave it a kick and Toots burst into tears.

CHAPTER SEVEN

~ Major F. ~

'Don't worry. I'll get it for you,' whispered Olive very quietly. 'Stay here.'

Silently Olive took her hoop of cobweb rope, then unhitched her bucket from her belt and handed it to Toots. 'Back in a jiffy!' she whispered as she flew up and disappeared into the smoke.

It felt to Toots that Olive was gone for ever. Over by the fire the Bocan smith had returned to his anvil and the air rang with clanging as he took to hammering again. Sedge, Loach and Bog Bean stood in a huddle arguing over a purse of money.

Toots watched them for a long time until eventually she saw the thin grey loop of cobweb rope drop through the smoke like a shadow and gently fall over the amethyst. None of the Bocans had noticed.

Toot clung to the reed and crossed her fingers as the ring began to rise silently out of the fire. She could see that the higher it got, the smaller it became. As long as none of the Bocans turned around, as long as none of them noticed, it would be all right. Toots's fingers hurt from being crossed so tightly and she could hardly bear to watch as the ring, half as big as it had been, now rose above the fire.

Without warning it shot up into the air as its gravity switched from the right side up world to the upside down one. Toots wanted to squeal with happiness, but she restrained herself. Suddenly she felt the strange fluttering at the corner of her vision again. She rubbed her eye.

'Toots!' hissed a voice behind her. 'Toots!'

Toots turned round. Rebecca's white face poked out through the reeds. 'Pike,' she whispered.

'Eel,' replied Toots, who hadn't expected to see her so soon.

'My boss, the major, wants to meet you. There's been another development. Climb down into the smoke then go two reeds forwards and four to the right.'

Rebecca disappeared. Toots hesitated. Olive would be back soon. But she had promised to help Rebecca; she couldn't let her down. Besides, it was all rather exciting, this sort of secret stuff. Toots quickly climbed down into the smoke and counted two reeds forward and four to the right, then waited.

'Pike,' said a voice in the smoke.

'Eel,' responded Toots again.

'Good. You came,' said the voice and out of the smoke a fairy's face loomed towards her. The fairy wore wire rimmed spectacles on her long thin nose and her wide mouth moved quickly as she spoke.

'There isn't much time. My name is Major F. Agent Watts tells me you're very clever. I hope you are. The situation is terrible. This much we know. The Bocans have taken the house fairies prisoner and are making them repair the cracks in the dam so that the Naiad will be safe when the weather breaks. It is sheltering in the shallows on the far side of the dam. The Bocans are protecting it until it is strong enough to climb above the dam and infest the whole river. Then everything will be poisoned. There is only one way to get rid of a Naiad. We must flush it out to sea. A Naiad cannot survive in salt water.'

'But how can you do that?' asked Toots.

Major F. shook her head. 'I don't know. If only the weather would break.'

'You mean if it would rain.' Toots's face lit up. She was pleased with herself for thinking of this so easily. 'Of course, the rain would fill the river and the dam would burst before the Bocans had had the chance to repair it and the evil Naiad would be flushed out to sea. Is that what you mean?'

'Yes, you are clever. Watts was right to trust you with

this.' The major's voice slid down another notch and she crooked her finger. Toots leaned in closer. 'We believe that the river fairies have something that can bring about changes in the weather. Whatever it is, they keep it secret. But we're sure they have it. And we have to get it from them.'

'Why don't you tell them about the emergency?' whispered Toots. 'Why don't you get them to call for the rains?'

'Because,' replied Major F., her pink tongue licking her lower lip. 'We have just learned beyond a doubt that Captain May, the river fairy captain, is one of them!'

Toots gasped, 'A Bocan?'

'No, an imp.'

'A marsh imp?'

'Sssshhhhhh!' hissed the major clamping her hand over Toots's mouth.

'Toots!' Olive's whispered voice echoed through the smoke. 'Toots, where are you?'

The lenses of the fairy's spectacles glinted in the dim light like two moons. She lowered her voice even further. 'Because she's a marsh imp the false captain will not call for the rains. Security in the river fairy headquarters is incredibly tight, but if we are to save the river, we must call for rain and we need the means to do so.' The fairy glanced quickly over her shoulder.

'Time is running out. We suspect that Captain May

knows we're on to her. That's why we need someone brilliant and unknown. Someone who that masquerading marsh imp won't suspect. Someone clever like you!'

'Toots?' Olive's voice hissed through the smoke again. Toots could hear her climbing through the reeds towards her.

The major leaned closer. 'Go now. Report to Watts if you find anything out. We're counting on you, Toots. Good luck. You're the bravest house child I've ever met. You won't let us down, will you?' she said as she disappeared into the smoke.

'I won't,' said Toots. Her head was spinning. There was so much to take in. There was an evil water sprite in the river and the river fairy captain was a marsh imp in disguise. It was awful. The Upside Down World by the river was in a terrible mess. Toots was glad that she would be able to help. It was exciting being trusted by Rebecca and the Special Forces. She only regretted that she was sworn to secrecy and couldn't share her burden with Olive.

A hand clamped around her arm. Toots jumped.

'Toots!' gasped Olive breathlessly. 'I've been looking for you everywhere. Couldn't you hear me?' Her face was red and sweaty, and smut from the Bocans' fire had dirtied her nose.

Toots shook her head. Olive handed her the saucer-sized ring.

'It's still shrinking. I think it's all right – it was only softened a little by the fire,' she said, untying the cobweb rope and handing it to Toots. 'It'll be the proper size for you in a minute.'

'Thank you so much,' said Toots slipping it on to her fattest finger, even though it was still as big as a bangle.

She watched as her ring shrank around her finger. She didn't know what she would have done if she'd lost it. She really didn't. It grew smaller and settled into place. Soon it was just as much too big as it should have been. Toots tried to smile at Olive, but Olive had her field glasses up to her eyes and was looking up towards the dam.

The evening wind had ruffled the reeds and had momentarily pushed away the heavy smoke from the Bocan camp.

Toots rummaged in her bucket and found her field glasses. She put them to her eyes. Then her mouth dropped open. All along the dam exhausted-looking house fairies, weighted upside down by heavy chains around their waists, were hammering at the wall. A group of Bocan warriors, heavily armed and brandishing whips, stood guard.

Toots was horrified and angry. This was all the Naiad's doing. Rebecca had said it had sent the Bocans to capture the house fairies and those foul creatures were making the house fairies repair the dam so that the Naiad would not be washed out to sea when the rains came.

'We have to do something,' whispered Olive. 'We have to get them out of there.'

Toots lowered her field glasses. What could two of them do against so many Bocans? Toots shook her head. Nothing.

She looked back into the camp. The curtain of smoke was falling back in place. The house fairies on the dam were already hidden from sight. Soon the Bocan camp would be obscured as well. Toots jutted out her chin. She would just have to do all she could to help Rebecca. She would find out all she could about the false Captain May, then they'd be able to save the river.

She suddenly had that strange feeling again. The fluttering at the far edge of her eye. Toots turned quickly to look, but again there was nothing beside her.

Olive tugged at her sleeve. Toots looked up at the Bocan camp and saw that a Bocan quite as ugly as the rest with a red patch across one eye was waddling quickly towards the fire. He spoke swiftly to every Bocan he met and pointed up into the reeds. One by one the Bocans turned towards the place where Olive and Toots clung to the reeds and glared at them with their piercing eyes.

'How on earth . . .' Olive hissed and grabbed Toots's

arm. 'They've spotted us. Let's go!'

In the camp the Bocans with bows were loading them with silver tipped arrows and those with swords were drawing them from their scabbards and advancing towards the reeds.

Toots suddenly realised that hanging from the reed as she was, there was nowhere for her to run so that Olive could pick her up and fly her to safety.

'There is another way,' said Olive urgently. 'I'll fly to the bottom of the reed, then you let go and I'll catch you.'

Toots didn't get a chance to hear this again because Olive had already flown off. Toots understood what Olive had said, but she couldn't seem to let go of the reed. She was paralysed with fear. If she stayed, the Bocan archers would pierce her with arrows, if she fell and Olive missed, she would tumble to the edges of the universe.

'Olive?' she cried. The Bocan archers were pulling back the strings on their bows.

'Toots!' shouted Olive. 'Quickly! Don't worry, I promise I'll catch you.'

Toots took one look at the advancing Bocans and let go of the reed. The Bocans and the reeds seemed to fly up away from her as she fell down towards the sky.

'Arrgggghhhhhh!' screamed Toots as she tumbled backwards.

'Oooomph!' cried Olive as she caught hold of Toots. the two of them rolled over and over as they fell into the sky. Fifty Bocan arrows sailed after them, but Olive and Toots flew faster. The arrows lost momentum and fell back towards the Bocan camp.

Olive banked around and landed on the broad branch of a nearby tree. It wasn't till she set Toots down and leaned exhausted against the trunk that Toots saw Olive was hurt.

'Olive,' Toots cried when she saw the torn sleeve and the red gash in Olive's arm.

'Just a scratch,' said Olive, pulling a leaf off the tree and tearing it into strips. She wrapped it like a bandage around the wound. 'I'll be all right,' she said, but she winced in pain.

'Olive, don't you think we ought to go to the river fairies and get help?'

Olive gave her a long look.

'What do you know about river fairies?' she asked. 'Was that cadet at the cottage talking to you about them?'

'No,' Toots lied, crouching down and busying herself with tying her shoelace. Toots didn't want Olive to see her face. She hated lying to Olive, but she couldn't break her promise to Rebecca. 'I just thought that we're near a river and perhaps they would help us. Especially now that you're hurt.'

Olive looked uncomfortable. 'Well . . .' She squirmed a bit. 'Well, to tell the truth I'm a little nervous of going to see them because, well,' Olive gulped, 'well . . . because I think they'll frown on me for being only a garden fairy. There's not much mixing in the fairy squadrons. It's not really done. I don't know if it's the same where you go to school, but for me I'd much prefer to visit the school I'm at or one I've been to, than the one I hope to go to in the future. I'd feel strange poking my nose in there. I'm much more comfortable with house fairies because I was one once, but river fairies? River fairies are the elite amongst the landed fairies, la crème de la crème. I hate to go bothering them.'

'But Olive, you need to get that arm looked at and maybe the river fairies will be able to rescue the house fairies.'

'Yes, I know you're right.' agreed Olive, pushing herself up off the branch. 'I was just being silly. Come on then, we'd better go before the sun sets.'

CHAPTER EIGHT

~ Captain May ~

Olive's injured arm made flying difficult and painful. Toots tried to ease her pain by holding on only to her good arm, but with every beat of her wings Olive winced. Bocan arrows sting worse than any nettle and, although the leaf bandage had helped a little, Olive's arm needed proper attention.

Olive flew bravely to the other side of the river where they hoped the reeds would be free of Bocan soldiers. As they flew close to the strange flat island, Toots looked up at the twisted mass of dark brambles and shuddered. In the evening light the island looked more sinister than ever.

Olive flew past it and up into the shelter of the reeds.

'Here, cling to this,' said Toots, helping Olive on to a reed by the water.

'If you tell me what to do,' said Toots, 'I'll call the river fairies and ask them to help us.'

Toots climbed on to the reed next to Olive's and

stared up at her own reflection in the mirror of water.

'Pat the surface with your hand. Three short slaps.' Olive told her. Toots reached up and did as Olive said. Three short slaps. Pat, Pat. Pat. She paused and waited. It was quiet on the river. Toots watched the ripples spread prettily out over the water, making her reflection waver and buckle.

'Olive, what do marsh imps look like?' asked Toots as she stared at the ripples.

'They can look like anything,' Olive replied. 'Anything at all. Underneath they look like imps: their skin is as red as cinnabar and their eyes are black.'

'But when they look like someone else you can't tell if they're imps or not, can you?'

'Pat the river again,' said Olive when the first ripples had died down. Toots did it again. 'No, oh except for one thing. There is always something red about them somewhere. It can just be a tiny speck but if you look carefully it's always there. The trouble is sometimes you don't get the time to look.'

Toots stared off at the river. She would have to be on the look out for something red when she met the river fairies' captain.

'Here they are,' said Olive.

It was then that Toots noticed the pondskater skating towards them. She'd seen these insects before, when she was the right way up, and had often watched them skimming over the river supported by the surface tension of the water.

At first Toots thought Olive meant that the pond-skater was one of the river fairies and it occurred to her that if this was so she wouldn't know what to say to Olive when she became a river fairy and turned into an insect. Toots's discomfort vanished as the pondskater skated right past them, but a second later, when a peculiar head popped through the water and gurgled something unintelligible at them, her discomfort returned.

The head was covered all over in a tight cap of mottled green and brown dappled here and there with patches of gold. The eyes were big and round and shiny like an insect's eyes and in its mouth it carried a mouth-piece from which two thick tubes floated into the water. Looking up through the surface Toots could see that the creature's body was covered in the same strange dappled skin as its head, and its feet were as large and as round as dinner plates with short tufts of hair at the edges.

'Hello there!' said Olive. Toots thought she was forcing herself to sound confident. 'We don't mean to bother you, but we need help. There's trouble on the land.'

The head bobbed twice and dipped back into the water. Toots hoped this was a friendly greeting.

Toots watched the creature in the water turn a

somersault then climb out of the water feet first down a neighbouring reed. It stopped when it was level with Toots and Olive, then grabbed its bulbous eyes with one hand and pulled them off its face. Toots winced as both 'eyes' came away (with a snap), then she laughed when she realised that the eyes were no more than a type of snorkelling mask and behind it was a sweet-faced fairy with merry brown eyes.

'Olive Brown!' cried the river fairy as she pulled the mouthpiece with the tubes from her mouth. 'Olive Brown, is it really you? I can't believe it.'

Olive's eyes opened wide in surprise.

'Nancy? Nancy Wren? Oh Toots, this is Nancy Wren,' said Olive beaming with pleasure. 'Nancy, this is my friend Toots. I knew Nancy a long, long time ago when I first became a house fairy cadet. She was just about to graduate and she showed me the ropes and looked after me when I was a hopeless novice fairy.'

'Tish!' said Nancy winking at Toots. 'Olive was always a very good fairy. The best cadet. You're a house child, aren't you?' she asked Toots, looking her up and down.

'Yes,' replied Toots.

'Thought so. What are you doing here?'

Toots was just about to launch into a long explanation when Olive cut her off.

'Nancy,' she asked suddenly serious. 'Do you know

what's been going on in the cottages along the river bank? All of the Upside Down Houses have been ransacked and the Bocans have taken all the house fairies prisoner.'

Nancy bristled. 'We know. There's trouble in the river too. Serious trouble, or we would have been up there to help out.' Nancy lowered her voice. 'We're pretty sure there are marsh imps on the island.'

Olive jerked when she heard this and the wound in her arm, which she had forgotten in the excitement of seeing her old friend again, twinged sharply. Olive winced.

'What's wrong?' asked Nancy full of concern.

Olive told her about the Bocan arrow and showed her the bandage around her arm. Nancy took charge.

'That needs a proper dressing on it. Can you swim?' she asked both of them.

Olive nodded. Toots did as well. She had learned to swim as a baby and was now in the swimming team at school.

'I've only got one spare mask though,' said Nancy, reaching into the pouch at her side and bringing out a set of tubes and buggy glass eyes.

'My training mask is in my bucket, if you could get it for me, Toots,' said Olive. Toots found the mask in Olive's bucket and brought it out.

Nancy spat into the eye pieces of the spare mask,

then reached up and dipped it in the water. She swirled the water around the glass then tipped it back into the river. The water flew up away from the masks.

'It stops the mask from steaming up,' Olive explained when she saw the perplexed expression on Toots's face.

Toots did the same to hers, then Nancy helped her put it on. The mask was a snug fit and the straps pinched her ears. Everything looked round and distorted through the bulbous glass eyes.

'Be careful,' Nancy warned her. 'Being this way up, strange things will happen to you in the water. Stay close to me. As you swim up towards the river bed gravity will try to pull you back towards the surface and if you give in to it, it will grab you and pull you out into the sky. Keep swimming and you'll be all right. But, and this is very important, when you come back to the surface swim slowly and zig zag through the water. If you swim fast, nothing will be able to stop you falling out into the sky.'

Nancy lifted up the mouthpiece with the strange ribbed tubes.

'Put this in your mouth. It's like a snorkel even though the free end doesn't stay out in the air. Water passes through it and it works like the gills of a fish. You'll find with a bit of practice that you'll be able to breathe easily. But try not to breathe through your nose or you'll steam up your mask and won't be able to see where you're going. Don't worry about swimming for the first bit, I'll pull you along, but don't forget to breathe whatever you do.'

Clinging to the reed with her injured arm, Olive reached into her bucket and pulled out two pieces of waterproof green material, and Toots, seeing what she meant to do, helped her fasten them over the tops of both their buckets. Then Olive folded her wings and waited while Nancy helped her tuck them into the opening at the back of her flying suit.

'Remember, Olive,' said Nancy as she fastened up the opening. 'It's dangerous to fly with damp wings. Always try and air them properly before you fly, won't you?'

'I will,' answered Olive. 'Fairies hate flying with wet wings,' Olive added for Toots's benefit.

'What happens when it rains?' asked Toots.

Olive and Nancy both shuddered.

'Flying in the rain is every fairy's nightmare,' they said together.

Once Olive's wings were safely tucked away, Nancy helped her pull the mask over her head and pointed up to the water. Olive nodded.

Nancy climbed swiftly up the reeds and, placing the mouthpiece in her mouth, entered the water making hardly a ripple. Olive was next. Nancy helped her through and then it was Toots's turn.

Toots put her mouthpiece in her mouth and climbed up the reed. She could hear her breath roaring in her ears. It was an uncomfortable sensation and it suddenly struck her that this was what it must sound like to be Robbie, always breathing noisily the way he did. Toots didn't like it and she felt a little sorry for him, but once she pushed her head up into the water she forgot all about Robbie and his noisy breathing because her first sight of the underside of the river made her forget almost everything.

Inside the glassy, bug-eyed mask her own eyes opened wide as she stared at the glorious silver surface of the water. Swirls of light danced over it in a gossamer screen and stretched away in all directions to the dark bank. Above her, light bounced across the river bed, glinting and flashing in sparkling golden ripples. Tench and sticklebacks slid in and out of the shafts of afternoon sunlight while beneath her, beyond the gossamer screen, the evening clouds drifted lazily across the sky.

Behind the constricting mask Toots could feel the muscles in her cheeks wanting to stretch into a huge smile. She had to fight the impulse because if she opened her mouth, water would seep in at the corners and she might choke. But then a sobering thought struck and stopped her smiling. If the Naiad was allowed to stay all this would disappear and the river would get choked up. The desire to smile vanished.

Olive and Nancy clung to their reeds waiting for her. Once she was in the water, they prepared to take off. Toots watched in amazement as Nancy stepped on to the underside of the water's surface and, balancing on her big circular flippers, swayed with the barely perceptible waves that moved across the water. She held out her hands; Olive took one and Toots the other. Then Nancy began to skate across the glassy underside of the water.

Toots suddenly found herself travelling at an incredible speed. Tiny bubbles covered every inch of her and tickled her skin. When she looked back she could see the elegant ripples Nancy made in the river, long graceful arrows cutting through the water. If her mouth hadn't been full of tubes, Toots would have squealed with joy.

When they reached the middle of the river, Nancy stopped skating and they drifted and gradually slowed to a stop. Toots realised that the only thing that had prevented them from falling out of the water had been Nancy's skill on the wide based skates. She would have been scared if she'd had time to think about this, but Nancy was signalling to her that they should now swim up to the river bed; this was no time for feeling frightened.

About thirty or forty metres above them a pipe lay along the river bed. Nancy kept hold of Olive's and Toots's hands and kicked her feet in the big round flippers vigorously. When they were a good five metres above the surface of the river Nancy let go of their hands and let them swim by themselves.

It wasn't all that easy to swim up to the pipe. Toots swam breaststoke with her arms and kicked with her feet, but her ears soon began to hurt the way they did when she dived into the deep end of the swimming pool to retrieve a penny from the floor. She tried not to think about it and concentrated instead on the pipe above her.

It was made entirely of crystal. Not bright sparkling crystal that has been cut and polished, but rock crystal rubbed smooth by the continual motion of the water. It was transparent in some places and cloudy in others, like an ice cube. The thick walls were full of striations that varied in colour from purple to pink to the palest blue. Some parts sparkled prettily in the last of the sunlight and it looked as though tiny shreds of gold leaf were caught in the stone. It was very beautiful.

In the distance she could see other crystal pipes branching off from the main one and disappearing into the reeds, or into the river bank, or right up into the river bed itself.

Olive tugged at her arm and Toots saw they had

reached a square opening or dock in the lower side of the main pipe. It was the size of a small swimming pool and its edges were crowded with fairies wearing masks and mouthpieces. Toots watched as one by one these fairies dived off the edge and shot through the water like rays of sunlight, each one hurrying in a different direction. She understood now why the river fairies' uniform was dappled with grey and brown and gold patches. It made them almost invisible as they swam up towards the stony bottom of the river.

Toots gazed fascinated as the fairies looped up and round the pipe and darted between the stones as though they were searching for something. Then she noticed other, stranger, figures on the river bed.

These figures must have been fairies because their diving suits and helmets were patterned in the same mottled design as Nancy's, but they didn't look much like fairies. They wore big round diving helmets which had thick, glass portholes in the front. Their diving suits were huge and baggy. Two long tubes were attached to their chests and led all he way back to the dock where two fairies wound a big wheel that made a pair of bellows go up and down. On their feet they wore great boots with thick metal soles.

But the strangest thing of all was that these fairies were walking with their heavy boots across the bottom of the river bed. They were the same way up as people and this meant that they were the wrong way up for fairies. Toots stared up at them. How could they be standing on the bottom of the river?

She didn't have any time to think about this. Nancy and Olive had reached the dock ahead of her and they were already climbing up out of the water. There were three steps into the tunnel and Toots slipped on every one of them which made her feel stupid, especially as there were a few river fairies staring at her. Toots kept her eyes on the floor while Nancy helped her off with her mask.

The crystal floor was clear here and it was like looking at the world through the bottom of a drinking glass. Everything was distorted and strange. Beneath her the sunset sprawled across the sky, pink and gold and turquoise, and the little waves on the river flashed silvery lilac in the fading light.

Toots looked up and felt nervous when she saw how large the little group of fairies had grown.

'Stop your staring, you lot,' said Nancy hotly as she shooed them away. 'There's nothing for nosy parkers here.'

The fairies fell back and went quickly about their business as Nancy pushed through, making a way for Olive and Toots.

Nancy sat Olive on a bench and helped her remove the sleeve of her flying suit. Gathering what she needed from a first-aid box she put some salve on the wound and dressed Olive's arm in a nice clean bandage. Olive felt and looked much better almost immediately.

'Right, let's dry you both off, then we'll go and meet the Captain,' said Nancy, helping Olive to her feet. She opened a door and led them both into a small room that was cut into the thick wall of the tunnel. At the far end of the room stood an enormous fan with crystal blades. Nancy hit a switch and the fan began to turn. Warm air rushed over them. Soon flying droplets of water were being blown off their clothes and were splashing the walls like rain against a windscreen.

In a few moments they were completely dry and Olive's face was red from the heat. Nancy led the way back out into the dock.

A fairy in heavy diving gear was being led down the steps into the river. Two fairies followed her, each of them holding one of the diver's heavy boots. The boots floated in the air, rising above their heads like helium balloons.

'The lead on the soles comes from your world,' whispered Olive.

'River fairies use it when they need to walk on the river bed. They don't put them on until the last minute because it's too uncomfortable for them.'

Toots nodded to show that she understood though she wasn't quite sure that she did.

'Where has everyone gone?' asked Nancy looking around at the nearly deserted dock.

'Those who aren't out searching are at an emergency meeting in the Captain's cabin,' replied the fairy, struggling with the boot as it threatened to pull her to the ceiling.

'Thanks,' said Nancy, then she beckoned to Toots and Olive. 'This way, we'd better hurry.'

The crystal tunnel shone with the many colours of the sunset as the little party hurried to the reeds in the distance. Toots gazed down through the partially transparent floor as she walked and watched the fishes and river fairies swimming beneath her feet.

She wondered briefly how it was that she could breathe in the tunnels and then in answer to her question, they came across several pale green and brown tubes that stood waist high in the corridor like narrow chimney pots. Toots stopped and peered down one and saw the pale evening sky, a little faraway circle of turquoise. The air tube was a hollow river reed. Toots took a deep breath. She could smell the river and freshly mown grass. It smelled of all her summer holidays rolled into one.

'Keep up if you can,' urged Olive in a whisper, tugging on Toots's shoulder.

Eventually the corridor opened out into a wide hall which was full of long, clear glass tables. Glass chairs were arranged neatly along both sides of the tables and places were set with glass plates and cups and transparent knives and forks.

As they passed through the dining hall, Toots noticed a long cabinet halfway along the wall. It was like a museum case with glass at the front and on the top and it was lined with purple velvet. At the front was a delicately wrought golden lock. Toots stopped to peer in.

There, neatly displayed on the velvet, was a blue feather, a shell, a grey pebble, a tiny tooth and a small, silver-banded horn with a small black leather book beside it.

'Olive?' hissed Toots forcing Olive to turn back. 'What are these for?'

Olive looked over Toots's shoulder. Her face lit up. 'Oh, I know all about these from my studies. They are the river fairy squadron's most precious possessions. They use these to look after the river. The feather is waved when they need to call a council of river birds. The shell is for when they need to confer with the fish, the pebble they tap when they have to discuss things with the frogs and toads and newts and tadpoles, the tooth brings all the insects together and . . .' Olive looked up anxiously to see that Nancy hadn't left them behind.

'What about the horn?' asked Toots suddenly

intrigued by these objects. 'You missed out the horn and the little book.'

Olive took her hand and led her away from the case.

'The horn is the most important tool of all. By blowing the horn the captain of the river fairy squadron can change the weather. The book contains instructions about the different notes she needs to sound for the different kinds of weather.'

Toots's eyes lit up. 'She can make it rain? Or be sunny? Or snow? Just by blowing that horn?'

'Yes,' replied Olive. 'But we don't have time to talk about it now. We have to follow Nancy.'

Toots bit her lip. Perhaps this was the very thing the Special Forces needed to call the rains and flush away the evil Naiad. Toots glanced back at the cabinet. If she could just get that little silver-banded horn and summon the rain, perhaps then she could save the river.

Nancy was already at the other side of the hall and was hurrying towards a small door in the corner. The door was made of dried river reeds which had been woven together. She gently slid the door open and held a finger to her lips to warn Toots and Olive to keep quiet.

It was hot and incredibly crowded in the small room beyond the screen. This was why the corridor and the dining hall had been so empty. Almost thirty river fairies were crammed into the small room. Some of them were even perched on the book shelves because there wasn't any room on the floor.

Nancy, Olive and Toots squeezed themselves in behind the outer ring of fairies. Toots found herself behind a tall fairy and she couldn't see anything at all. She could hear someone speaking at the front of the room.

'That's Captain May,' whispered Nancy, pulled Toots over a little so that she could see better.

Toots stood on tiptoe and craned her neck to see over the crowd of fairies. Then her heart stopped.

Captain May stood at the front of the room facing the assembled fairies. She was a small, sweet-faced fairy with a body as round as a beach ball. Her head was round as well and so was the bun that wobbled on top of her head. She looked like a three-tiered cottage loaf and just as sweet as any fairy leader anywhere, but her cheeks were as red and as bright as two cherries.

Toots looked around at the river fairies who were listening with big believing eyes and at Olive who was obviously smitten with everything about the river fairy squadron, and she was flabbergasted.

How could they look at the captain and not know that she was a marsh imp in disguise? It was so obvious. Even if Rebecca hadn't warned her, Toots would have known.

Toots listened carefully to the captain's speech,

growing angrier by the minute.

'We must find the Naiad,' said Captain May thumping her hand down on the desk. 'As you know, searches continue for her around the clock; the fish have joined us and are helping in every way possible, but there is no sign as yet.'

The fairies groaned.

Toots frowned. The captain had managed to make them think that they had to protect the Naiad. She had made them believe that the Naiad was a good thing for the river. Toots glanced at Olive. With all her studying surely she should have known that the fairies weren't supposed to protect a Naiad. Hadn't Rebecca told her that no river fairy wanted a Naiad in her river?

The Captain clapped her hands for silence.

'There's bad news with the Bocans as well, I'm afraid.' She lowered her head and raised her eyes. 'We don't yet know for certain who has brought them to the river, though we have our suspicions. As we learned last week, the Bocans are using the house fairies to break down the dam.'

Rubbish, thought Toots outraged. It's the exact opposite. The Bocans are trying to repair the dam so that the Naiad won't be washed away, but will stay and poison the river. Toots narrowed her eyes. The captain was still speaking. Toots listened harder.

'You all know that if the dam breaks, there's a distinct danger that the Naiad, wherever she is, will be washed out to sea. Under no circumstances can this be allowed to happen.

'It's beginning to look more and more likely that the Bocans have captured the Naiad and have hidden her somewhere. Finding the Naiad must be our number one priority. The Bocans may have managed to trap her on the far side of the dam, in which case she will be suffering dreadfully in this awful drought. All attempts to see if she is on the other side of the dam have so far been thwarted by the Bocan archers, but we must and will get through. To this end we will be arranging a high altitude aerial attack. Lieutenant Wren, will you see to that, please?'

Captain May looked around the crowd. Nancy raised her hand and nodded.

'Good, we'll discuss it after the meeting,' said Captain May. 'As soon as we know where the Naiad is and can make her safe, we'll be able to try to free the house fairies from the Bocans. One last thing. As you all know, it's more than time for the rains. I know this is hard for all of us, and that the river is very low, but I cannot risk summoning the storm before we have made certain that the Naiad is safe. For this reason the horn will not be blown and the summer storm not sum-moned until we've found the Naiad.'

Toots scowled at the captain. All these lies, she

thought. All these awful lies. She looked around at the river fairies and felt so sorry for them. They seemed to believe everything their captain said. Toots couldn't understand why no one smelt a rat. It seemed so obvious to her, but then she was privy to secret information. Toots wished again that she could tell Olive what Rebecca had told her. It would make the burden so much easier to bear.

The reed screen doors were pulled back and the river fairies filed out. Toots was right in their way and would have been carried through with them had not Olive pulled her back into the room.

Soon the room was empty and only Nancy, Olive, Captain May and Toots remained. Captain May was wearily sorting through her papers.

Nancy stood in front of her and saluted.

'Ah, Wren, at ease,' said the Captain, lowering herself into her chair and clasping her chubby hands over her round stomach.

'What news?' she asked, her eyes opening extra wide as she noticed Toots and Olive. 'Hello, who are these two strangers?' she asked in a kind and welcoming voice.

Nancy beckoned to Olive and Toots to step forward.

Olive stood to attention and saluted.

Captain May listened intently while Olive told her where she had come from and all about Toots and about the deserted Upside Down Houses and the Bocan camp and the house fairies who were imprisoned and being made to knock holes in the dam.

When Olive had finished the captain put her hands flat on the desk and stood up.

'Thank you, Cadet Brown,' she said in a sad voice. 'I take it you heard most of my speech just now. Do you know what the Naiad is?'

'Yes, ma'am.' Olive took a deep breath. 'The Naiad is the guard . . .'

The captain smiled and held up her hand. 'It's all right, Cadet Brown. You don't have to recite your entrance exam here. 'Yes, ma'am' will suffice. This is all so dreadful. You heard that the Naiad is missing. We've searched all over the reservoir and not a sign have we found. I can only think that the Bocans have captured her and hidden her somewhere. We must find her. I hope to goodness that she is all right.' Captain May pinched the bridge of her nose between her thumb and forefinger.

Toots looked up. Olive didn't seem to register that this was not the sort of thing you would expect a River Fairy Captain to say.

'I didn't say this at the meeting because I didn't want to discourage the others, but we're pretty sure that there are marsh imps behind all this,' said Captain May, struggling to maintain her composure. 'Ruddy marsh imps trying to take over my river! Their scouts have been spotted on and around the island. That's no doubt what they're after. It's muddy enough for them. They're probably planning to drain the reservoir and take over the island after they've flushed us out. Marsh imps on my river! Ugh!'

Toots watched the captain closely. Rebecca had warned her that she might try this. It was a clever trick to pretend that you were shocked by something that the enemy did so that everyone thought you were what you said you were. Captain May was clever, very clever, but Toots wasn't fooled.

The captain looked at Toots. She had very intelligent eyes and she seemed to see right through her. The captain smiled. Toots noticed that she had a kind smile and was glad that she had been warned about her. If she hadn't been, she might have thought that the captain was actually quite nice.

Captain May sighed, then turned to Olive and took a deep breath.

'I'm afraid you'd better take Toots back where she came from. It's likely to get too hairy here for house children. Especially if there are marsh imps and the Bocans involved.'

Toots was mortified. How would she be able to save the river if Olive took her home?

'How's your swimming?' the captain asked Olive.

'Not bad, ma'am,' Olive replied respectfully.

'Arm not bothering you?' Captain May nodded at the bandage.

'No, ma'am.'

'Good. As soon as you've taken Toots home, you can return here and join the group who are scouring the northwest bank.'

Toots was too stunned to protest. She looked at Olive. Olive was so besotted with the whole idea of being a river fairy that she couldn't see what was happening either. How could everyone be so wrong?

The Captain dismissed them and stood up. 'Lieutenant Wren? The charts for the current current flow if you please.'

Nancy waved a quick goodbye to Toots and unfurled a sheaf of papers on the captain's desk. Soon both of them were lost in a complicated chart that was covered in arrows and different coloured wavy lines.

Toots's face was flushed and hot as she followed Olive out of the door. Captain May was a horrible imp and if Toots hadn't promised Rebecca, and didn't know that doing so would jeopardise the entire mission, she would have shouted that fact at the top of her voice till it echoed long and loud through the tunnel.

CHAPTER NINE

~ Going Home ~

All Toots had wanted to do was help the fairies. She had hoped that she might be able to do something to help them get rid of the Naiad. Surely they wanted to get rid of it, didn't they?

Perhaps they had all been bewitched by Captain May. As Toots and Olive crossed the dining hall, Toots wracked her brain as to what she should do. She didn't want to let Rebecca down. She had promised to help.

Then her eye fell on the cabinet against the wall and she remembered the little silver-banded horn. If she could just take that and give it to Rebecca then Rebecca would be able to summon the storms that would wash the Naiad out to sea.

Toots didn't want to steal. It felt wrong, but if she was being sent home, what else could she do? She had to help in any way she could. She made up her mind. If she could get the horn to Rebecca, that at least would be something.

Now she had to think of a way to get it without Olive seeing her.

As they passed the cabinet, Toots slipped her amethyst ring off her finger and let it drop to the floor. She coughed to cover the noise it made as it clanged against the crystal. Olive didn't hear it. Toots followed Olive back towards the dock.

When they were halfway down the corridor and almost at the air tubes, Toots pretended that she had just noticed the ring was missing.

'Olive,' she called as she ran back towards the dining hall. 'I lost my ring. I'm going to look for it. Wait for me!'

She passed Nancy on the way back, but she didn't stop. She just called over her shoulder where she was going and didn't wait to hear what Nancy said about it.

Toots was breathless when she reached the dining hall and her heart was thumping like a drum in her ears. She was feeling desperate enough to run right up to the cabinet, break the glass and steal the horn, but just as she turned the corner she stopped and hung back. Someone was standing by the open cabinet. It was Captain May and she was holding the little silver-banded horn in her hand, balancing it on her palm as though she was trying to guess its weight.

Toots could hear the captain talking to herself. She strained her ears and listened.

'Not yet,' said the captain holding the horn against her chest. 'The fish will have to do without fresh water for a little while longer. We must protect the Naiad. Without the Naiad our river will die.'

The captain put the horn back in the cabinet, then, after closing and locking the lid, she walked back into her cabin and slid the door shut behind her.

As soon as the coast was clear Toots hurried across the dining hall and scrabbled for her ring on the floor. She found it and slipped it on her finger then dashed over to the cabinet. She was trying in vain to lift the locked lid when the door to the captain's cabin opened and the captain stood framed in the doorway blinking at Toots.

Toots leaped back and stumbled against a chair.

'I'd lost my ring,' she blurted, trying to explain. 'I must have dropped it and now I've found it.' The captain looked puzzled. 'Bye then,' cried Toots, not waiting for the captain to start asking questions. She just turned and bolted along the long corridor towards the dock.

Olive was waiting for her and helped her on with her mask.

'I'm sorry you have to go home, Toots,' she said and Toots knew that Olive meant it. 'But I'll come and see you when this is all over. Try and remember to leave your ring box open so I can get back to my garden squadron with you.'

Toots nodded, but she wasn't really listening. She was angry with herself for failing in her mission and she was trying to think of something, anything, she could do to make it all right.

She hardly noticed the river as she and Olive swam back to the surface. The sky beneath them was almost dark; only a few turquoise streaks remained in the west.

The swim back was easier. Her inverted gravity pulled her down towards the surface. They swam slowly in a zig zag pattern. Toots remembered Nancy's warning about how if she wasn't careful she could be yanked right out of the water and into the sky. If that happened she wouldn't stop falling till she reached the edges of the universe.

Toots was careful. When she was only a few feet away from the surface she turned a somersault and trod water with her feet pointing down towards the sky.

Now that the sun had set the water was dark. It was like floating in a pool of warm ink. The moon had not yet risen and the only light on the water came from the reflections of the yellow lamps in the cottage windows. These danced and skittered across the waves, but did not penetrate far into the water.

Toots could hardly see two metres in front of her, and it was a relief when Olive loomed out of the darkness and took her hand to lead her to the surface. But suddenly the world erupted into a million bubbles, as though someone in the right side up world was running through the shallows, kicking their feet, splashing and churning up the water.

Before they knew what had happened, or had time to react, Toots and Olive were engulfed in the foam. The violent waves of the runner's wake swept them away.

Toots felt Olive's grasp on her hand slip and Olive's shadowy outline vanished in a cloud of gold rimmed bubbles. Within seconds Toots was lost in the churning water. Over and over she rolled through the froth.

She didn't stop rolling until she reached the reeds. Toots bounced from one thin stalk to another until the rush of water died down and she was able to grab hold of one of the reeds.

As the bubbles dispersed, Toots found herself alone in the dark water.

CHAPTER TEN

~ Sally Greenteeth ~

Toots clung to the reed. 'Where is Olive?' she wondered. 'Is she all right? What if the bubbles have knocked her out of the water? Her wings are tucked up behind her. She won't be able to fly.' Toots clung more tightly to the reed. She couldn't think like that. Olive would be all right, of course she would. Olive would be coming to look for her as soon as she could. Toots knew that. But then a frightening realisation came to her. How would Olive ever find her in the dark?

Toots looked down. The sky was getting lighter where the full moon was rising behind the trees. Occasional silver ripples twinkled below her. It occurred to Toots that Olive probably wouldn't try to look for her in the water, but would more than likely dry out her wings and then fly over the river to search. It would certainly be faster than swimming. Toots nodded to herself. That was what Olive would do. She climbed swiftly down the reed and out into the evening air.

Toots pulled off her mask and took out her mouth-piece, then stowed them neatly beneath her bucket's waterproof cover, marvelling as she did so at how much the bucket would hold.

She shivered and her teeth chattered. She was cold and wet and lost. She looked miserably at the reeds all around her. Their tall straight stems reached up into the water and down towards the sky. Looking down Toots began to feel a little seasick watching their ends waver in the wind. Perhaps her idea had not been such a good one. How would Olive ever find her in a forest as dense as this?

Toots's teeth chattered and she shook the water out of her hair to stop it from dripping into her eyes. She realised with a gulp that she would have to climb to the bottom of the reed if she wanted Olive to be able to see her at all.

Slowly and steadily Toots climbed down the reed's stalk. As she climbed, the moon appeared below the tree tops and cast an eerie light over the river. Toots was grateful to be able to see where she was going, but the light was so cold and uncomfortable that part of her would have preferred stay in the dark. She comforted herself with the thought that at least Olive might be able to see her when she flew by.

Toots reached the bottom of the reed and her heart fell. It was so much shorter than its neighbours. She couldn't see over the tops of the other reeds. She was no better off than she had been up by the water.

She clung to the reed and wondered what she ought to do next. Returning to the water was the only solution she could think of and that was not much good. Toots groaned.

Her groan turned into a scream as the warm evening breeze suddenly blew through the reeds shaking them this way and that. Toots wrapped her arms and legs about the reed and screwed her eyes shut.

When she thought she had been swung as far as the reed could bend in one direction the breeze suddenly changed its course and just for fun blew her the other way. Toots opened her eyes and screamed again as the reed pushed back into its neighbours. It was lucky that she opened her eyes just then, because if she hadn't she wouldn't have seen the thick stalk of the reed mace which stood like a pillar, tall, firm and unbending in the wind, while the thinner reeds quivered around it. Toots had seen reed maces from the river bank. They stood higher than the reeds, tall and straight, their thick, long, brown, cigar-like pokers crowned with a waving feathery spear.

Toots didn't have time to think about the danger. She didn't have time to think about what would happen if she missed the reed mace and fell into the sky. She only had time to act.

Toots leapt.

The impact of the reed mace against her chest winded her, but Toots hardly noticed. She grabbed the thick stalk and clung to it for dear life. Her heart was pounding in her ears as she gasped to recover her breath.

She stared down at the sturdy trunk of the reed mace. Now she could see its long brown seedhead beneath her sticking out below the tops of the other reeds. If she climbed down to it, there was a good chance that Olive would be able to see her.

The reed mace was so thick, it only quivered slightly when the wind rushed through the reeds and Toots was able to climb down it quickly and easily.

The reedhead's base was wide enough for Toots to sit on. She looped her legs around the stalk and sat down. Above her, beyond the reeds, the river swirled silent and silver in the moonlight. But the moonlight on the water did not seem pretty to Toots. It seemed sinister and dangerous.

Desperately she scanned the river for Olive, but there was no sign of her. On the far bank the yellow lights burned in the cottage windows. They seemed very far away and suddenly Toots felt lost and alone in the world, like someone from another planet.

From the reed mace she could see all the river. She could see the dam and hear the faint sounds of the fairies' hammers as they were forced to repair it. She could see the ripples in the water where it was draining into the sluice at the far end of the dam.

In the reeds by the bank, beyond the sluice, she could just make out the pinprick lights of the Bocans' fires through the acrid smoke that settled over their camp. And on the far side of the dam she could see the shallow backwater that the stream from the sluice never reached.

Perhaps Rebecca would come, she thought. It seemed odd that she hadn't. Perhaps she was too busy. Toots stared up at the river and doubt began to creep into her mind. What if Rebecca was wrong? What if Captain May really was Captain May and not a Marsh imp? It suddenly seemed strange to her that Olive should have been fooled. And all the other river fairies too. Perhaps it was Rebecca who was wrong. Perhaps... The more Toots thought about it the more the doubts seeped in.

She shook herself. The dark and the cold were getting to her. She gazed over at the strange, stagnant backwater on the far side of the dam. There the stones were smothered in blanket weed.

In the eerie light the blanket weed, ghastly and grey against the dark shore, seemed to move. The stark shadows made the rocks beneath the weed look like slumbering creatures. Toots shivered. Perhaps it was just a trick of the light. Then one of the rocks began to move and, like someone awakening from a deep sleep, it slowly turned a ghastly slime-smeared face towards her.

Toots wanted to look away, but she couldn't. She was transfixed. Two horrible hollow eyes stared at her and a mouth as black as soot opened in the distorted face and moved up and down as though it was calling to her. Pond slime dripped from the mouth. A weed-draped arm, thin as a spear, rose up and a long-fingered hand reached for her as though it would grab her and pull her down into the hideous mouth. But she was too far away and it could not reach her. The hand dropped back into the stagnant shallows.

Toots screwed her eyes shut and buried her face in her shoulder. 'Sally Greenteeth! Sally Greenteeth!' screamed a voice in her mind and she wished Luke hadn't tried to scare Robbie with horrible tales.

When Toots dared to lift her head again the shallows beyond the dam were just as they had been before. The awful head and the raised arm had sunk back in amongst the stones. Toots breathed again. Then suddenly a shiver ran up her back and shook her to her bones.

Of course, she thought, that creature, that apparition, that terrible thing, was the Naiad. It had to be. This was the thing that Rebecca had said was destroying the river.

All her doubts vanished. Now she knew that Rebecca had been speaking the truth, for how could anything so terrifying bring anything but harm to the river?

Toots suddenly saw the fluttering at the edge of her eyes again and swung around, but again there was nothing.

'Pike?' said a voice in the reeds.

'Eel,' Toots was about to reply, but before she could, the heavy Bocan manacle closed around her wrist and the weight of it pulled her arm sharply up towards the river.

CHAPTER ELEVEN

~ Bladderwort the Vain and Terrible ~

Toots had been so lost in thought that she hadn't even noticed the reed mace quiver as the three Bocans climbed up it.

The Bocans reeled her in.

Toots was terrified. 'OLIVE!' she yelled, as the Bocans pulled her up towards the water. 'OLIVE!' she cried again. But Olive didn't come.

At close quarters the Bocans were more terrible than anything that Toots had ever seen. She felt sick as they glowered at her with their vile eyes and she could hardly breathe because of their horrible, overpowering, obnoxious odour. Toots narrowed her eyes and stared up at the three Bocans above her. They were the same three that had stolen her mother's ring.

The Bocans not only looked more horrible close up, they were also much bigger than they'd seemed from a distance. The smallest one was twice as big as Toots. Struggling or fighting would be pointless.

'Told you we hadn't got all of 'em,' snarled Loach as he pulled hard on the chain.

'No you didn't,' whined Bog Bean. 'I said we hadn't and you said we had and now here I am proving you wrong.'

'Shut up and keep pulling,' snapped Sedge.

As soon as she was within reach, Bog Bean grabbed Toots, and, stuffing her under his arm like a newspaper, climbed down onto the back of an unhappy looking toad where the other two Bocans were waiting.

The toad was obviously a prisoner being forced against its will to carry the Bocans. Toots felt sorry for it. A heavy Bocan bridle was strapped tight about its nose and a mantle of chain and leather hung over its back.

Loach kicked his heels deep into the toad's knobbly flanks. The toad began to paddle miserably through the reedy shallows.

'S'like carrying nothing at all,' said Bog Bean hitching Toots up under his arm. 'Fairies! Huh,' he grunted, 'easier to catch than measles.'

'Not as much fun though!' snorted Loach, cracking his whip sharply across the toad's nose.

Sedge gave them both a filthy look. Loach and Bog Bean travelled the rest of the way in silence.

Toots was extremely uncomfortable. The heavy chain clanked against her arm and she felt as though she was being bounced black and blue.

Fortunately the journey didn't take long because the toad swam quickly. In less than five minutes it leapt up onto the river bank and waddled across the mud to the edge of the Bocan camp.

The Bocans dismounted and marched through the reeds towards the light of the smoky fires.

As Bog Bean entered the camp carrying Toots under his arm, all the Bocans turned and stared at her. Some of them laughed.

'That's a weedy 'un, Bog Bean,' guffawed one.

'Call that a fairy, it's nobbut a runt if *you* can carry it,' scoffed another.

Bog Bean vibrated with anger. He tightened his grip on Toots and, drawing his sword, turned to rush at the jeering Bocans. Sedge held him back.

'Not now,' he hissed through gritted teeth. 'You can fight later!'

Bog Bean jerked his neck twice and pushed his sword back into its scabbard. He hitched Toots up under his arm again and carried on his way.

The three Bocans marched through the camp and entered the biggest tent.

Once inside, Bog Bean let Toots go and she shot down and bounced at the end of the chain half a metre short of the ceiling. The manacle chafed and pulled against her wrist.

It was hot in the tent. So hot that Toots's clothes, which were still wet from the river, began to steam. A great fire roared in a long flat stone hearth in the centre of the tent and black smoke streamed up towards the hole in the middle of the ceiling.

The air in the tent was foul and thick and Toots coughed on to the back of her free hand and stared though the flames.

Bog Bean pulled on the chain attached to Toots's wrist and dragged her after him into the heart of the tent. He wasn't very careful with her and didn't notice when she disappeared into the clouds of smoke above the fire. Toots came out the other side coughing and spluttering and with a face covered in soot.

She rubbed her grimy eyes and blinked at the brightness.

At first she thought that there was a grand display of mirrors in the tent all reflecting the bright fire, but then, as her eyes grew accustomed, she saw that they weren't mirrors. They were weapons, bright, gruesome weapons, of every imaginable type.

Everywhere she looked highly polished swords and spears and arrows glinted fiercely. Broadswords lay fanned out on the floor, spears stood behind. Short swords were stacked with silver spiked maces and axes with jewelled handles stood upright beside golden crossbows and catapults.

At first Toots didn't see the creature lounging on a dais surrounded by the dazzling display, but when she did her stomach turned.

This Bocan was the largest she had ever seen and his boils were more lurid and more plentiful. His skin was pink like the other Bocans', but a green and lumpy mould like the kind you find on stale bread had blossomed on his cheeks and forehead. His nose was scarred and swollen. His mouth was wet and glistened like a fresh wound and a white salty crust of spittle gathered in the corners. His chin was covered in long, greasy hairs which were too few and too far apart to be called a beard, but which were nevertheless combed and oiled and curled.

The most terrifying thing about this Bocan were his eyes. They were colder than a witch's heart and they were filled to the brim with a calculating greed.

Though revolting in his body, this Bocan wore the brightest armour of all. His mail was made of small, gold, lozenge-shaped leaves which moved when he moved and sparkled in the light. On top of this he wore a golden chest plate engraved with fine patterns and encrusted with jewels. By his side rested a helmet of silver and gold.

This Bocan paid no attention to the little party that stood before him nor to the girl who hung at the end of the chain with her feet pointing towards the ceiling.

This Bocan was busy smoothing out the long wiry hairs on his chin with one hand and twisting a tiny dagger in the other. He was trying to catch his reflection in the narrow blade, but he was far too fat to see more than a quarter of his nose in such a tiny mirror. With a growl he threw the dagger down and picked up a short broadsword which was much better suited to the job.

Bog Bean, Loach and Sedge got down on their knees and bowed. The enormous Bocan still took no notice, then Bog Bean coughed politely and he reluctantly turned his terrible head away from his reflection and stared down at them with contempt.

'What?' he said with enormous impatience.

Sedge was the only one who dared to speak. His voice quavered.

'Oh great Bladderwort, Vain and Terrible as you are, we humbly bring this . . . this . . .'

Bladderwort the Vain and Terrible glanced at them and then at Toots with a look of pure disgust.

'Well? What is it?' he demanded in a voice like thunder. The gold leaves of his chest plate trembled.

'A . . . a . . . fairy,' stammered Loach, grabbing the chain that was attached to Toots and jiggling it.

Bladderwort rolled his horrible eyes. 'Why did you bring it here? Put it to work with the others.'

'This one's different,' offered Bog Bean, his voice higher than a choirboy's.

'Different?' roared Bladderwort. 'What do you mean different? Can she work or can't she? Can she move dirt or not?'

'Yes, probably . . . I think so . . .' began Sedge. 'But she doesn't smell the same as the others.'

Bladderwort threw back his head and sniffed. The bushes of black hair in his cavernous nostrils shivered like sea grass in a storm.

'Hmm!' he said, reaching for the little bow at his side and fitting an arrow into it. 'Maybe this one's just for sport.' And he aimed the arrow right at Toots.

Toots wriggled on the chain in an attempt to avoid the arrow and as she did, the fire-light caught the amethyst ring on her finger and made it sparkle. Bladderwort's greed was such that, even surrounded by gorgeous and glittering wealth, he could not see a jewel or an ornament that belonged to someone else without wanting it desperately. He lowered his bow.

'What's that?' he hissed pointing to the ring. His sharp eyes glinted fiercely in the light.

Toots knew immediately that he was talking about her amethyst. She bunched her fist and shoved her hand in her pocket.

'I want it!' snarled Bladderwort sitting up.

Bog Bean pulled on Toots's chain and she began to rise to the Bocans' floor, Toots wriggled and kicked and squirmed and twisted, but nothing could stop them from pulling her up. Soon her head was dangling close to their stinking mud floor.

Bog Bean and Loach hung onto the chain while Sedge fumbled with her arm and tried to force her to take her hand out of her pocket.

They were taking too long. Bladderwort grew impatient. He stood up, his gold armour clanking and rattling, and staggered over to her. He snorted through his nostrils as his horrible slimy hands grappled with her arm. Toots screamed as her hand was pulled out of her pocket and her arm was twisted behind her back. Bladderwort prised her fingers open one by one until he found the ring.

When he did, his fat fingers snatched it from her.

'No!' cried Toots as the ring slipped off her finger. Bog Bean and Loach shoved her away and let her fall back to the end of the chain.

Toots screamed as she shot back down towards the ceiling. Losing her ring was the last straw. But she stopped screaming when she saw the rip appear in the ceiling below her.

'Olive?' cried Toots. 'Oliv –' But it wasn't Olive. Toots gasped as Rebecca's dark curly head and white, white face popped through the hole.

'Pike!' she said with a wink.

'Eel,' replied Toots. Toots looked at the Bocans. None of them had noticed.

Bladderwort was too busy admiring his new ring. He popped it on to the end of his littlest finger and held it up to the light, twisting it around to make it sparkle.

Bog Bean, Loach and Sedge didn't hear either. They were too busy smiling ingratiatingly at Bladderwort and hoping that he would reward them now that he had what he wanted.

'Toots!' mouthed Rebecca. 'Take this.' Rebecca pushed her arm through the hole she'd made in the tent and passed a skeleton key up to Toots. But it was just out of Toots's reach. She was hanging at the very end of the chain and if she strained to get the key, she would remind the Bocans that she was there.

Acting quickly Toots gritted her teeth and grabbed the key between the soles of her feet. Then, concentrating very hard, she brought her knees up and with her free hand grasped the key. It was only when she jiggled it in the lock that Bog Bean noticed what was going on.

'Stop!' he shouted. But Toots only twisted the key harder. All at once the lock opened, the manacle released her and she fell to the ceiling in a heap.

Above her, Loach and Sedge fell on to the floor as the heavy chain dropped on their heads. Bog Bean quickly drew his bow and aimed his arrow at Toots. But before he could fire, Rebecca pulled her through the hole.

Toots screamed as she dangled dangerously down towards the sky. Looking up she saw that Rebecca was holding her by one leg and pulling her towards the reeds. Bog Bean's arrow whizzed by her ear. Toots was surprised by how immensely strong Rebecca was for such a little fairy.

'Quick, latch on to this reed, and follow me,' shouted Rebecca. 'We'll have to move fast to get away from them.'

Toots did as Rebecca suggested and soon the pair of them were climbing swiftly from reed to reed in an effort to escape the pursuing Bocans.

It was hard going but soon they were lost in the forest of tall reeds and the lights of the Bocan fires were far behind them.

Rebecca stopped. Her pale face glowed like a ghost's in the moonlight.

'I think they've given up,' she panted, staring back at the distant fires. 'Are you all right?'

Toots nodded. Then after a pause she added, 'Thanks for rescuing me.'

'You're welcome,' replied Rebecca. 'We like to keep an eye out for our operatives. Especially our bravest ones.'

'I really thought Olive would have come to find me,' said Toots staring up at the black water that swirled about the reeds.

Rebecca sighed and looked a little embarrassed. 'I think she stayed with the river fairies.'

Toots nodded. 'Of course,' she said with a twinge of disappointment. Olive couldn't come and look for her because she had her duty, hadn't she?

'Did you have any luck up there?' asked Rebecca cocking her head towards the river. 'Did you find out anything that might help us.'

'Oh? Oh yes,' replied Toots forcing herself to stop thinking about Olive and looking up at Rebecca. She told Rebecca everything she'd seen in the river fairies, headquarters, about Captain May and her rosy red cheeks and about the way that she had persuaded all the river fairies to think that the Naiad was not evil but good and needed to be protected.

Rebecca shook her head sadly.

'But that's not all,' added Toots. Rebecca looked up. 'There was one thing I thought might be useful. A small, silver-banded horn that Olive told me can be used to change the weather. If you blow it in a certain way, it will bring the summer storms.'

The whites of Rebecca's eyes gleamed in the moon-light.

'That's it,' she gasped. She grabbed Toots's arm. 'That has to be it! Toots, you are so clever. Summoning the storm is the only thing that will rid us of the Naiad. We must have that horn, Toots. We need you to go back and get it for us. Please say you will. We're all counting on you. You must do it.'

Rebecca was squeezing Toots's arm so hard that it hurt. Toots pulled away. Rebecca remembered herself.

'Sorry,' she said, a little embarrassed. 'It's just that I am so keen to get rid of that thing, I get a little over-excited. Here, take this.' She pressed the bone-thin skeleton key back into Toots's hand. 'It might open the cabinet.'

Toots looked at the key in her hand.

'What do you think, Toots?' hissed Rebecca in the moonlight. 'Can you go back and get that horn so that we can save the river? Can you?'

Toots looked at the dark swirling water and remembered the thing she had seen rising out of the blanket weed. She didn't want the river to be ruled by the Naiad. She looked down at the bright circle of the moon.

'Yes,' she said closing her fingers about the key. 'I'll do it.'

'You really are so brave,' smiled Rebecca stroking Toots's arm better.

CHAPTER TWELVE

~ The Thief ~

Toots fished in her bucket, brought out her mask and slipped it over her head.

She had no idea how she was going to find her way back to the river fairies' headquarters, or steal the horn from the cabinet, but she knew she had to try. She'd promised Rebecca and she couldn't let her down.

'I'll be waiting for you. Good luck, Toots,' whispered Rebecca with a wave as Toots climbed up the reed towards the black water.

Toots slipped the goggles over her eyes and put the mouthpiece in her mouth. Doubts ran through her mind helter skelter as she climbed into the dark water, but one look at Rebecca's face told her that she couldn't go back on her word. Rebecca was counting on her to save the river and the house fairies.

The water was cool and dark and still as Toots swam up towards the river bed. It would have been faster, she knew, if she'd been able to skate across the surface the way that Nancy had done but for one thing she didn't have any skating flippers and for another she didn't know how to do it. She couldn't risk falling over and breaking through the surface of the water.

A great ghostly trout loomed out of the darkness like a silvery submarine and shocked Toots as it passed by her. Its glassy eyes gleamed in the refracted moonlight. Toots's heart beat loudly in her ears and she had to try twice as hard to stop thinking how frightening it was to be alone in the dark water.

She forced herself to concentrate on swimming up towards the river bed. Soon she could see the lights from the river fairies' crystal tunnels in the distance. Toots began to feel a little better. At least now she knew she was heading in the right direction. If she could reach the tunnel, she was almost certain she could find her way to the dock.

Presently she was able to see other lights in the water and she soon realised that they were the fairies' phosphorescent torches. There seemed to be dozens of fairies, as though the entire river fairy squadron was out searching for the Naiad. Perhaps they were all out and the headquarters were empty. That would certainly make it easier for her to take the horn unnoticed.

Toots swam up close to the crystal tube and by pressing her mask up to the cool stone could see the blurred but unmistakable shape of Olive walking along the corridor inside.

Toots banged on the stone, but it was obvious that Olive couldn't hear her. Olive was going somewhere in a hurry. Toots felt betrayed. Rebecca had been right. Olive hadn't bothered to come looking for her when they'd been separated. She had simply returned to the river fairies.

Nancy joined Olive on the corridor. Toots wished that she could hear what Nancy was saying, but the stone was too thick. Whatever it was it had an effect on Olive. She broke into a jogging run and Nancy trotted after her. Toots tried to follow them. She kicked her legs as hard as she could and tried to keep up, but she couldn't swim as fast as they could run and she soon lost them.

Toots could see the dock now a little way ahead. She could see through the crystal that there were hardly any fairies there and it would be relatively easy to sneak in unnoticed.

As she reached out onto the first crystal step and popped her head out of the water, Olive and Nancy reappeared. They had their masks on already. Toots hid close to the steps as they sat on the edge of the dock and fixed their flippers to their feet. Now she could hear what they were saying.

'We haven't looked over by the dam yet,' said Olive.

Toots noticed that there was a great deal of anxiety in her voice and she looked worn out. 'There are a lot of reeds over that way. Perhaps she's lost in there. Oh, I only hope we find her before it's too late.'

Nancy nodded. 'Don't fret, Olive,' she said. 'We'll swim there together and then split up. We're sure to find her. Be on the look out for the Bocans though.'

Olive's face grew pale. 'Oh Nancy,' she said with horrified eyes. 'You don't think . . .?'

Nancy shook her head. 'Don't worry, Olive. We'll find her. Keep your chin up.'

Olive nodded, then pulled her goggles over her eyes. Nancy did the same and as soon as they were ready they slipped into the water. Toots watched as they each lit an underwater torch and then, carrying them high, swam swiftly away.

Olive was searching for the Naiad with Nancy. She was too busy trying to be a river fairy to have the time to search for Toots. It hurt her to think that Olive had forgotten about her. Toots frowned and the rubber at the front of her mask puckered. She didn't see why Olive was so enamoured with the river fairies. They weren't very nice at all. Toots remembered how much nicer Olive had been when she was a house fairy and felt sad to think that one day her friend would be a stuck up river fairy who would be too busy to have time for her.

Now the dock was empty and Toots knew that she had to act fast. She lifted herself out of the water and pushed her goggles to the top of her head. Spitting out the mouthpiece she looked around. All was silent and still. The only sound was the water dripping off her clothes on to the floor. Toots stared down the long, long corridor, past the ventilator pipes to the dining hall in the distance where the horn was kept. She saw that the coast was clear and ran as fast as she could down the crystal corridor leaving a trail of wet foot-prints on the floor behind her.

She was breathless when she reached the dining hall and her heart was thumping in her ears. She was breathing loudly as she fumbled with Rebecca's skeleton key in the lock of the cabinet. Through the glass she could see the silver-banded horn and the little book of instructions.

It opened more easily than she thought it would, but when she lifted the glass top the hinges creaked loudly. Quickly Toots reached in and grabbed the little horn and put it in her pocket. Then she swiftly rifled through the black leather book.

It was a dictionary of various types of weather. It would tell her what notes to blow on the horn. Hurriedly Toots looked under s for storm and read through the list.

'Hail storm . . . Storm clouds . . . Spring Storm . . .

Summer Storm.' That was the one she wanted. She turned to the page indicated. 'To summon the summer storms,' she read, running her finger along the words, 'blow one long, low note. A long, low note as sad as the end of summer.'

Suddenly the door to Captain May's cabin slid open and Captain May herself came out. Toots dived beneath the cabinet still holding the little black book in her trembling hand. Her heart thumped in her ears, but she knew she hadn't been seen.

Captain May stood with her hands on her hips staring suspiciously across the dining room.

'Who's there?' she asked. When nobody answered her quick eye fell on the cabinet. She marched over to it and when she saw the empty space where the horn and the book should have been she gave a little shriek.

'Gone!' she cried. Her tiny feet danced back and forth, then one foot found the puddle of water that Toots had left on the floor. The captain pawed it with her toe. 'Intruders,' she whispered to herself. 'Imps?' She barely dared to breathe the word. 'Sound the alarm,' she suddenly cried in full volume. 'Sound the alarm! We must protect the Naiad wherever she is!'

The captain hurried over to a small, glass-fronted, red box on the wall and, taking off her shoe, punched a hole in the glass with the heel. Inside was a large button and the captain pushed it as hard as she could. At once the dining hall was filled with a flashing red light and a hideous siren began to wail.

Toots looked up in a panic. Beyond the semi-transparent walls of the dining hall she could see the lights of the fairies' phosphorescent torches in the water. The red light was summoning them all back to headquarters. Toots knew she would have to act fast. She did the only thing she could. She ran.

Still clutching the little book in her hand, she leapt out from beneath the cabinet and ran as fast as she could down the still empty corridor.

'Stop!' screamed Captain May when she saw her.

But Toots didn't stop. The red lights flashed and the siren wailed, and Toots ran on and on down the long corridor, her wet feet slipping on the smooth crystal floor. Captain May chased after her.

Through the murky crystal walls of the tunnels Toots could see the river fairies speeding through the dark water towards the dock to head her off. Toots ran faster. She knew that this was her one chance to help Rebecca. She knew what she had to do. She had to get the horn and the little book to her friend. She had to help her save the river from the marsh imps.

By the time Toots reached the dock it was crowded with wet river fairies who were climbing out of the water, pulling off their masks and looking about themselves to see what was going on. All of them looked anxious and alarmed.

'What's happening?' asked one as Toots, red faced and out of breath, charged through the throng. Toots didn't have time to answer.

'Stop her!' cried the captain who ran some way behind Toots, but her voice was drowned out by the wailing siren.

Nothing was going to stop Toots. She was determined to get past the fairies and out into the water. She hadn't considered how she would outswim the fairies once she reached the river. She would deal with that when the time came. For now she had to fight her way out of the dock. She had to do her duty; Rebecca was counting on her. She had to defeat the shape shifting captain of the river fairies.

Toots was lucky. She had the advantage. The river fairies were out of breath from their hurried swim and the loud siren and flashing lights were confusing them. Toots seized her chance and pushed through the crowd.

She pulled down her goggles over her eyes and fixed her mouthpiece in place as she ran.

'Stop that house child,' cried the captain as loud as she could above the noise of the siren. 'Stop her, she's stolen the horn.'

The fairies in the dock suddenly understood. Every one of them tried to grab Toots as she passed, but their hands were still wet and slippery from the river and they couldn't get a hold on her. Toots dodged past them and, suddenly finding herself at the water's edge, didn't stop to consider what she was doing, but jumped right in and swam away from the fairies' tunnel as fast as she could.

Toots had never swum so fast in all her life. She pumped her arms and kicked her feet and shot down through the inky water towards the night sky. She only looked back once. The sight of the river fairies swarming after her through the water was enough to spur her on. Judging by the number of torches, all the river fairies had jumped back in the water and joined in the chase. Toots's heartbeat thudded in her ears as she swam faster and faster.

It wasn't until she was just a few metres from the surface that she realised she wasn't going to be able to stop. She suddenly remembered the warning that Nancy had given her when she had first taken her to the river fairies' headquarters. She had been told that gravity would try and pull her up towards the surface and that if she wasn't careful she would be pulled right out of the river. Toots realised now why she had been able to swim so fast. It was because she'd been heading straight down towards the sky and gravity had indeed been helping her. Now nothing would stop her from falling through the glassy surface of the river. The bright moon rippled beyond the waves and Toots plummeted towards it.

But just as she burst through the surface, two of the masked and flippered river fairies caught her sharply by the ankles and pulled for all they were worth. Toots spat out the mouthpiece and screamed as she jerked to a halt. The top part of her body hung out of the water, waving to and fro like a ragdoll. The jolt was such that the little instruction book flew out of her fingers. It shot into the sky, its white pages fluttering as it vanished into the night. Suddenly she felt sick. The sight of the little book disappearing so rapidly into the abyss reminded her how far she would fall if the fairies, who had hold of her, let go.

Toots craned her neck and looked up through the water. The two fairies were paddling for dear life and trying to pull her back into the water, but her weight was too much for them and as she jerked down another notch or two, she could tell they were losing their grip on her ankles. Suddenly she slipped through their fingers and out into the night.

She screamed for all she was worth as she tumbled out of the river and down into the sky.

CHAPTER THIRTEEN

~ No More Secrets ~

Over and over Toots fell, arms flailing, legs waving as she plunged towards the bright circle of the moon. In some ways it didn't feel as though she was falling, but as though the dark world was rushing up away from her.

She stopped screaming as she fell past the tree tops; there didn't seem to be any point. Screaming wasn't going to help. Who would be able to hear her? Now there was only the sound of the night air rushing past her ears and beyond that there was a great and terrifying silence. Above her the moonlit river twisted across the dark landscape like a silver ribbon. Wisps of clouds brushed past her through the chill night air and Toots grew cold.

But she wasn't afraid. To her surprise she suddenly felt strangely calm and extremely clear-headed. It was as though all her fear had left her, as though she had suddenly realised that there was nothing she could do to change what was happening to her.

Soon, she thought, I'll fall out of the sky altogether and perhaps right out into space. Toots stared up at the world. The river was now only as thick as a piece of silver thread and it was impossible to pick out the lanes or houses in the countryside. Somewhere up there her father was fast asleep.

Suddenly she felt sorry that she'd put a pillow in her bed to make it look as though she'd run away. Her father would never know what had really happened to her. And Olive, what about Olive? She would never know how Toots had tried to help the river fairies or why she had stolen the horn. Now the evil Naiad and the marsh imps and the Bocans would take over the river and the fairies would be driven away.

She blinked back the tears that welled in her eyes. The cold night air screamed in her ears and Toots shivered. She had failed in her mission and she had ruined everything for everybody. She stared up at the world. It was dark and distant.

She couldn't bear to look any longer. Then, as she turned her face away, she suddenly noticed the faint red shadow fluttering at the farthest edge of her eye.

Toots turned as if in a dream to look at it, but, as she did, something caught her around the middle and stopped her from falling. In the silent night Toots could hear only the rush of air beneath the beating wings. She twisted round and gasped with horror when she saw the huge damselfly that was clutching her tight with four of its six legs. Red fire flashed around the tips of its four enormous wings and shone in the many lenses of its bulbous eyes.

Toot closed her own eyes, but images of being eaten slowly by the sharp mandibles plagued her so she opened them again and blinked up at the dark world as the damselfly flew swiftly towards it.

Soon she could see the moonlit river and the cottages and, before long, the reeds and the dam and the ripples on the water. Perhaps the damselfly was taking her to its nest, or lair, or whatever damselflies had, and was going to eat her there slowly and with relish. Toots didn't want to be eaten. She would rather have fallen all the way to the edges of the universe, but from the way the damselfly was holding her, she knew she had no say in the matter. Toots stared up forlornly at the familiar cottages and trees. Perhaps this was the last time she would ever see the river.

'Goodbye,' she said to the trees as the damselfly flew past. 'Goodbye, Olive,' she added as she stared up into the murky depths of the river. 'Goodbye, Dad,' she barely whispered as she passed the last cottage in the row where her father was asleep.

But the damselfly didn't eat her. It flew past the dam towards the far bank then it dropped its head and flew into the reeds. It seemed deliberately to push her against a reed so that she could take hold, for when Toots reached out the damselfly let go and flitted away into the night. Toots clung to the reed. She was so shaken that she hardly noticed the red shadow fluttering yet again at the corner of her eye.

A rough tug on her sleeve made her turn. Rebecca's face was only inches from her own.

Toots jumped so much that she almost let go of the reed and fell into the sky again.

'It's all right,' said Rebecca grabbing hold of Toots's wrist. 'You're safe now.'

Toots stared at Rebecca. The outer edges of her black hair seemed to be tinged red in the moonlight. Rebecca quickly ran her hand through it and any hint of red disappeared. Toots wondered if it had ever been there in the first place.

'Did you get it?' Rebecca asked conspiratorially. Toots nodded and, reaching into her pocket, pulled out the little silver horn. Rebecca smiled and a strange little hiss of glee escaped from her lips.

The silver bands on the horn glinted prettily in the moonlight, but as Rebecca reached out to touch the horn the silver momentarily reflected a narrow red hand instead of her own white one.

Rebecca snatched her hand away quickly as though the horn was too hot to touch.

'Did you find out how to summon the storm?' she asked recovering herself.

Toots narrowed her eyes. 'One long, low note, a note as sad as the end of summer,' she said watching Rebecca closely.

Rebecca smiled. 'You'll get a medal for this,' she said with a cheery smile. 'You'll be famous, a legend for saving the river. Why don't you go ahead and blow it?'

Toots stared at her. Rebecca looked the way she'd always looked. But Toots couldn't help feeling uneasy. Now that she had the horn, now that she and Rebecca could call for the rains and flush the evil Naiad out of the river, Toots didn't feel right about it.

Something felt wrong. Very wrong. It was as though everything she had done with and for Rebecca had been against Olive and the river fairies. It was all very well to be involved in secret services, but she would have felt so much better if she could have talked to Olive about it. Now she bitterly regretted having made such a solemn promise to Rebecca. Now she wished she could have told Olive everything.

Rebecca seemed to sense her discomfort.

'It's all right, Toots. I'll do it if you don't want to. I just thought that you'd like to save the river. It's a big responsibility, I know, and if you can't . . .'

Toots looked at the horn in her hand and closed her fist around it. Why was she feeling this way? She had no reason to, she was sure of that. But she couldn't seem to shake the uneasy feeling.

Rebecca lowered her voice and stared over at the place where the Naiad hid in its lair of blanket weed. 'I only thought you'd be better at blowing it than me because you're so much braver.'

Toots swallowed hard. In the backwater the Naiad was rising. Its horrible hand was reaching towards her again as though it would pick her up and crush her in its slimy green fist. Toots quailed when she saw it. Rebecca was wrong. She wasn't brave. She was a big coward and she would much rather have been any-where but there right at that moment.

'Please,' urged Rebecca. 'Please, Toots. One long, low note. Or it will get us. Please.'

Toots lifted the horn to her lips. The Naiad reached out with its fingers stretched towards them, as if it wanted to pick them off the reeds and destroy them. Toots knew that it was time to act. She took a deep breath and rested the horn against her lips. Then drowning out the doubts that screamed in her head, Toots closed her eyes and blew one long note as sad as the end of summer.

When the note ended Toots opened her eyes and saw the Naiad collapse. As it sank down, the weeds fell away from its hollow eyes and instantly Toots knew she had done exactly the wrong thing.

The air grew thick and heavy. A warm wind sprang up and shook the reeds. The storm was coming. On the horizon there was a flash of lightning and a few moments later the thunder roared. The red shadow fluttered in the corner of Toots's eye again.

She turned to catch it faster than before. Rebecca stood there with a strange smile spreading over her face. Toots frowned. Red flashes danced all over Rebecca's body. They flew from the tips of her fingers and sparkled in her hair. Rebecca started to laugh. Red fire flashed in the darkness and suddenly the truth hit Toots like a slap in the face.

Of course. Rebecca, not Captain May, was a marsh imp.

Toots hung her head. Now the truth glared at her. Why had she not seen it before? But she knew why. It was because she hadn't wanted to see it. Because she had wanted all the stories about a secret service to be true. Because Toots had been flattered when Rebecca had wanted her to help, to spy, to steal. Toots was thoroughly ashamed of what she had done, but it was too late now.

Rebecca's laugh echoed through the reeds. Her innocent fairy eyes suddenly stretched as big as bowls and slipped on to the side of her head. Then her head flattened and grew wide and became the head of the damselfly that had saved Toots from her fall.

And then the shapeshifting imp turned into Major F. and then into the Bocan soldier with the scarlet eye patch and Toots saw how she had been fooled again and again and again.

The imp's head changed back into Rebecca's grinning one, then still laughing she pulled the tatty fairy uniform clean off and instantly changed from a fairy into a little wiry creature with skin as bright and as red as blood. Toots stared at its cruel face. Its bulging black eyes had no whites around them and in its wide mouth sat two rows of sharp yellow teeth. Its matted, pale, straw-coloured hair stuck up in tufts all over its head. Its hands and feet were long and bony and its leathery scarlet skin that shone like a well polished shoe was stretched so tight that it looked as though it might split at any moment.

Its eyes, dark and unfathomable, looked Toots up and down with a scornful gleam.

'Oh Toots,' laughed the imp in a scratchy mocking voice. 'You are brave, oh you are clever, oh, oh, oh. Only the bravest . . . oh ho ho.'

Toots caught her breath suddenly remembering all the awful things she had done at Rebecca's request. How could she have been so stupid? Toots knew then that everything Rebecca had told her was a lie just like Rebecca herself.

Toots thought back miserably to the first time she'd

seen Rebecca and remembered the uncomfortable feeling she'd had. Now she realised that every time she'd had that strange fluttering in her eye Rebecca had been there a moment later in one of her disguises. Toots groaned. She should have taken more notice. She should have listened to Olive's advice. She should have paid attention to her instincts. But she'd been too ready to believe in secret missions and finely spun lies.

The marsh imp crossed its skinny legs around the reed and, hugging its skinny shoulders, rocked back and forth snickering.

'How gullible you are,' it sneered. 'So eager to please. You thought you were so special, but you're not. Now, of course, you'll be famous.' The marsh imp snickered. 'Don't look so shocked. You wanted to do something that everyone would remember. And you've done it. The fairies here will always remember you as the interfering house child who stole the river fairies' horn and blew it so that the rains would wash the Naiad away. Oh, but I forgot, there won't be any fairies left to remember you so I don't suppose you'll be all that famous after all! There'll only be marsh imps on this river. Won't that be marvellous?'

The marsh imp grinned its wide leathery grin and showed all its spiky yellow teeth at once, then it shrieked and flapped its thin red arms and began to change again.

'I must go,' it said gleefully as dark blood-coloured fur bloomed suddenly all over its body and leathery wings unfurled from its arms. 'My friends will be impatient to move to their new home once those fairies are out of the way.' The marsh imp clasped its skinny red hands together and vibrated with glee. 'In fact,' it added, tapping its long fingers together in excitement, 'I think we might all come and watch the fun. It promises to be quite a show.'

It flapped its dark red wings, stepped off the rock and, with a last mocking wave, flew off toward the dark flat band of the bramble-covered island in the middle of the river.

Toots was more than miserable. Misery was where the feeling she was feeling began, but where it ended she had no idea. It was somewhere deep and dark inside her in a place where it felt as though nothing in the world would ever be right again. How could she have been so stupid, so gullible? How could she have believed such a ridiculous story?

She looked again at the Naiad lying sorrowfully in the blanket weed. The dark open O of its mouth no longer looked terrifying. Toots knew now that it hadn't been trying to hurt her. It had been reaching out for help. The Naiad no longer looked evil or menacing, it just looked pitiful and lost. Toots shook her head. She'd been so wrong. The Naiad wasn't evil, it was good. It was the sacred guardian of the river.

Toots's tears dripped toward the moon. She had ruined everything for the river fairies, for the house fairies and for the river. Soon the storm would come and the river fairies and the Naiad and perhaps the house fairies as well would all be washed out to sea.

CHAPTER FOURTEEN

~ Oh, Olive! ~

Toots didn't see the river black and beautiful above her and she didn't see the moon far, far below. She could only see her own sad thoughts. She could only see the trouble she had caused for everyone.

The same thoughts cycled round and round in her brain and she could think of nothing else. Why didn't she listen to Olive? Why had she let herself believe in Rebecca? Why had she been so gullible?

If only she could do something that would make it right. If only . . . oh, she was so cross with herself. Hot tears blobbed out on to her cheeks. Toots buried her face on her knees and sobbed.

The lightning cracked open the distant sky and the thunder rumbled. The storm was getting closer. Toots lifted her head. The warm wind grew stronger and rattled through the reeds.

Toots was still clutching the little horn in her hand and the wind was blowing through it and making a low moaning sound. Toots opened her hand.

Perhaps there was a way to send the storm back, she thought, looking at the horn. But even if there was, the instructions on how to blow it were written in the little book and that was lost in the limitless depths of the sky.

In the silences between the thunder she could hear the fairies on the dam being driven harder by the cracking whips of the guards. She could still hear the chink chink chink of their hammers as they chipped away at the dam, weakening it so that it would burst when the rains came.

Toots grasped the horn. There had to be something she could do. She could try blowing anything, but she'd already made one awful mistake – who knew what might happen if she tried a different note. If only Olive was with her, she'd know what to do.

She thought fondly of Olive even though she'd been cross with her the last time she'd seen her, even though Olive had stuck to her duty instead of coming to look for her. Toots knew that Olive would have come if she could. It was probably that Captain May who had forbidden her to look for Toots. Toots stopped and shook her head.

None of this was right. That was the way Rebecca or rather that horrible marsh imp had wanted her to think. That had all been lies. Toots thought about what she had heard Olive say when she'd last seen her in the river fairy HQ and her words came back to her. 'We haven't looked over by the dam yet,' Olive had said. 'There are a lot of reeds over that way. Perhaps she's lost in there. I only hope we can find her before it's too late.'

Now Toots realised with a pang that Olive hadn't been searching for the Naiad, she'd been looking for her. Toots felt terrible.

If only Olive was with her, she thought again. Olive would know what to do.

Toots lifted her head. Surely it would be worth trying to call Olive. Perhaps if Olive heard her she would come and do something.

Toots cupped her hands around her mouth and, directing her voice up to the waters above her, she shouted. 'Olive, Olive, Olive.' But her voice was lost in the roar of thunder. The wind blew harder through the reeds and made them rustle. Then the rain began to fall. Big single drops at first that flew up past Toots and plopped into the river like stones.

Toots saw that her voice would not carry very far against the wind. She remembered Olive's megaphone; perhaps there was a similar one in her bucket. Toots rummaged in it and soon pulled out a bright green one. She put it to her lips.

'Olive! Olive! OLLL-LIVE!' she cried as loud as she could, but even though the sound echoed over the river

Olive did not come. The rain fell faster and the sound of it hitting the river roared in her ears. Toots stared at the rain as it flew up into the water. It was strange to see it fall this way and it started to make her feel as though she was sinking down, as though the reed to which she clung was moving and the rain was standing still.

Lightning ripped across the sky and lit the whole of the river in a flash. The thunder roared. Toots lost heart. How would Olive ever hear her? Then it came to her. Olive could still be under the water. No wonder she hadn't heard her call.

Toots climbed up the reed and carefully leaned out over the rain dappled river. Raindrops the size of melons splashed all around her and one broke on the back of her head soaking her hair and dribbling down her collar. Toots shook it off and set the big end of the megaphone against the water.

'Olive! Olive!' she shouted. 'It's me, Toots. Olive. Can you hear me?'

The reed to which Toots clung grew slippery in the rain and she didn't know how much longer she could hold on. She had to try again. She had to.

'Olive,' she cried through the rain. 'Olive, it's me, Toots, I made a horrible mistake. Please come and help. The Naiad needs your help. She's here, on the other side of the dam. I need your help too, Olive. I'm sorry I messed up. It would be so good if you could come and I promise I won't do anything I'm told not to do again, but if you don't come now . . . if you don't come now . . . oh, OLIVE!'

Toots lost her grip and slipped down the reed. She tried to find her footing again but her feet just skidded on the wet stalk. She wrapped her arms about the reed and clung to it. She let go of the megaphone and it dropped into the rain and disappeared into the dark night sky.

Toots clutched the reed so tight that it felt as though her arms might break. Olive hadn't heard her. No one would come and help her now. No one would save her. Soon she would slip all the way down to the sky. The reed was too wet to hold on to for long.

The wind pushed against the reeds, bending them flat. And as they sprang up again Toots lost her grip and slipped all the way down to the very tip.

'OLLLLL-LIVE!' she screamed as the reed burned against her hands.

'It's all right. I've got you!' said Olive, catching Toots just before she fell.

CHAPTER FIFTEEN

~ Olive Takes Charge ~

Olive carried Toots towards the dam and a few moments later put her down in the shelter of a little cave where the Bocans had knocked out a brick. The river swelled black less than a metre over their heads and the raindrops splashed them as they hit the water.

'Now then, I've been looking everywhere for you,' said Olive looking seriously at Toots. 'What's been going on?'

'Oh Olive,' cried Toots, hugging her big friend around the middle and bursting into tears again. 'I am so sorry. I messed up everything.'

'It's all right,' said Olive as she gently pulled Toots away and crouched down to be on the same level. 'Everyone makes mistakes. You'd never learn anything if you did everything perfectly all the time, would you?'

Toots shook her head and wiped her eyes with the back of her rain-soaked hand.

Olive smiled at her. 'That's better. Now as quick as you can tell me what happened.'

Toots felt terrible confessing all her idiotic behaviour to Olive, but as soon as it was done she felt better. When she had finished, Olive didn't say anything, but stood staring out over the black water looking very severe. Toots wondered if Olive would still want to be her friend after all the stupid things she had done. Olive turned and smiled at her.

'You're not the first to have been fooled by the marsh imps, you know,' said Olive standing up. 'They are very devious and persuasive. I'm just cross that I didn't spot Rebecca for what she was either.' She looked up at the damage to the dam. 'But this is no time to be thinking about who's to blame. Where's the Naiad?'

'In the shallows on the the other side,' answered Toots pointing downstream.

Olive fluttered her wings. 'I'll just go and see. Back in a minute.' With that she ran to the edge of the brick and took off.

Lightning lit up the sky. The storm was getting closer. Toots stood alone and stared out at the river. Even though Olive had tried to make her feel better, nothing could. Toots knew that for the rest of her life she would regret that she had blown the horn.

Olive soon returned. Her face was very worried.

'Oh dear,' she puffed a little out of breath. 'The Naiad must have been out of the water for a long time. She's very weak. We'll have to act fast or we'll certainly lose her.'

Olive looked around the little cave as though searching for inspiration. She stared up at the black water. 'We won't be able to stay here for very long, the way this water is rising. I'll call the others and try and think of something to do. How many Bocan soldiers would you say there were?'

Toots tried to remember. 'Forty or fifty, I think. I didn't count them, but there were a lot. And you saw how well armed they were.'

'Yes, they were, weren't they?' said Olive as she climbed up towards the water. Toots watched her friend as she leaned out and patted the water with the flat of her hand. Olive slapped the water continuously as though she was beating a drum. Toots doubted that anyone would hear above the roar of the rain and the terrible thunder, but within less than a minute a dozen masked heads popped through the water. The fairies were all cadets; there were no officers so Olive took charge.

'You,' she barked pointing at one cadet. 'Find Lieutenant Wren and tell her to meet me by the broken part of the dam with as many cadets as she can muster. Tell her we've gone to free the house fairies and we may have a battle on our hands.'

'You,' Olive pointed at another. 'Get to Captain May as fast as you can and tell her that marsh imps are set to invade once the dam bursts. The Naiad is weak and unless we help she'll be washed out to sea when the waters break through. Tell her we're going to need all the help we can get if we're going to do battle with the Bocans and rebuild that wall before the river swells too much. Tell her she may need to call all the river inhabitants to an emergency conference. Now go. Anyone you see on the way, send them up here. The rest of you can climb onto this platform. We're going to see if we can't do something to free the house fairies and stop the Bocans breaking down the dam.'

When Olive turned back to Toots her face was flushed and excited. She gave Toots an 'I can't quite believe I'm doing this' sort of look, then her expression changed to one of great seriousness as the river fairies assembled around her.

Some of the river fairies weren't too happy to see Toots. She could tell by the looks they were giving her that they knew if they lost the river it was all her fault. And they weren't too pleased about a garden fairy, never mind a garden fairy cadet, telling them what to do. They began to mumble and mutter under their breath.

'You're just a garden fairy,' said one.

'We ought to wait for an officer,' whined another.

'There isn't time!' replied Olive forcefully. 'If we wait you might lose the Naiad forever.'

'Cadet Brown is right,' said Captain May stepping forward and pulling off her mask. In all the excitement no one had noticed the row of little gold stripes on the band of her mask. 'I'm going to take Brown's advice and call an emergency conference of all the inhabitants of the river. I have to return to headquarters to do this and until Lieutenant Wren arrives, Cadet Brown is in charge. Do you understand?'

'Yes, ma'am,' replied all the river fairies.

'Good. Carry on, Brown.'

Captain May replaced her mask, climbed back up the rock and disappeared in to the water. Olive saluted stiffly then took a deep breath and faced those who were now officially under her command.

'You're going to need your wings,' she said sternly. The river fairies bristled and eyed the rain. Olive noticed their expressions, but she wasn't going to stand for any nonsense. 'I know it's dangerous, but we have no choice. It's either fly in the rain or not at all. I hope you all still remember how to use your wings?' The fairies nodded and began to help each other to unpack them through the backs of their wet suits. Before long every river fairy was fluttering her wings to knock out all the creases and as soon as they were ready they stood to attention and waited for Olive's next instruction.

'We're going to launch a surprise attack on the Bocan warriors who are guarding the house fairies,' she whispered, pointing down to the top of the dam. 'Then we're going to work as quickly as possible to repair the damage that's already been caused.'

'The rain will work in our favour in one way,' Olive continued while the fairies got themselves into a line. 'The Bocans really don't like getting wet. This weather will be making them pretty miserable and they won't be at their full fighting strength.

'Everybody ready?' The river fairies nodded. 'Then let's go. Safe flying everyone.' Olive turned to Toots. 'We'll lead the way. Start running and I'll pick you up.'

'Are you sure you want me along?' asked Toots so quietly that only Olive could hear. 'I won't just be a nuisance?'

Olive rolled her eyes. 'Get going,' she said.

Toots ran across the slippery stone and just as she reached the edge, Olive flew over her and picked her up. They flew out into the rain and the rising black waters of the river swelled and swirled above them.

CHAPTER SIXTEEN

~ Freeing the Fairies ~

It wasn't easy flying through the rain and Olive soon needed her arms to help her balance. With one hand Olive passed a rope under Toots's arms, then threw it around her back and over her shoulder. Skilfully she caught the loose end with her teeth, then tied it in a knot. It was an awkward business and Toots thought more than once that she was going to fall.

The rain came down in sheets. Within a few seconds all the river fairies were soaked through and their wings were heavy with water. Each raindrop that hit Olive drove her up towards the river.

'Come on,' cried Olive trying to sound confident. 'We're not on a picnic. We're a rescue party. All fairies together.'

This spurred the river fairy cadets on and they shook the raindrops off their wings and flew as fast as they could.

All of them were a little shaken when they saw the

dreadful state of the house fairies, weighted to the dam as they were with the heavy Bocan chains. The house fairies were hanging by their waists with their feet pointing down towards the sky and their heads close to the dam so that they could reach up and chisel away at the rock. They were so exhausted that they seemed hardly able to lift their hammers. Toots wondered if the house fairies would be much good if it came to a fight with the Bocans. They all looked so worn out.

When the river fairies reached the reeds at the far side of the dam Olive beckoned to them to crowd around her. Then counting them off she separated them into groups of three. Each group was instructed to attack one Bocan. Olive held up her arm and mouthed one, two, three and on the third stroke she dropped her arm as a signal for the fairies to attack.

The crashing thunder drowned the sound of their approach and four of the five whip-cracking Bocans, who would rather have been sweating in their smelly beds than out getting washed by the downpour, never knew what hit them.

The first group of river fairies flew up behind a grisly looking Bocan and while one fairy snatched the whip from his horrible hands, the other two took his bow and arrows and threw them away. The Bocan was helpless without his weapons and though he struggled like a trapped bear he had no chance. The three river fairies caught hold of his hair and pushed and pulled him over the edge of the dam. The Bocan screamed blue murder as he dropped into the water.

When the imprisoned house fairies saw what was happening they suddenly livened up and with renewed energy swung on their chains towards the Bocans and joined in the fun.

Just one Bocan escaped. He had a dagger hidden in his belt and as he twisted himself free of the fairies' hold on his hair, he lunged at them with it. Then, realising he was outnumbered, he ran off towards the Bocan camp moaning and nursing his sore head in his hands.

'Let him go,' said Olive as two river fairies started to fly after the fleeing Bocan.

'But won't he warn the others?' asked Toots, who was afraid that all the other Bocans would come and attack them as soon as they knew that the house fairies had been set free.

'Yes,' replied Olive cryptically. 'But it'll take them a while to prepare to attack us. We have a little time.' Olive waited until the Bocan was almost out of sight then she turned to the river fairies. 'I need a volunteer,' she said. All the fairies flew forward. Olive pointed to one. 'Follow him to the camp and report back to me as soon as you can. I want to know exactly what they're doing. The rest of you, we've a lot of work to do here.

Come on.'

Olive flew over to the house fairies and explained the situation.

'I'm afraid you'll have to keep your chains on for a while,' Olive warned them. 'It's the only safe way that you can repair the dam without falling into the sky. As soon as everything is safe and we're sure the river can't burst the dam, we'll fly you all back up to your houses.'

The house fairies bucked up visibly.

In a matter of moments a plan of action for the emergency repairs on the dam was agreed and it was already underway when Lieutenant Wren arrived with about forty river fairies, all of whom were very surprised to see a garden fairy running the show. Some of them were even a little put out and began to mutter amongst themselves.

Nancy soon put a stop to that. 'Hush your noise, please,' she said. 'The only way we're going to save the river is if we all work together. I think Olive's done an excellent job so far. And Captain May has given her her full authority.' The river fairies held their tongues.

'Any news on getting extra help?' asked Olive nodding up to the river.

Nancy's face brightened. 'The captain was talking to the fishes when I left and that looked promising, and most of the amphibians, the frogs and so forth, are helping out with the rescue of the Naiad, though some of them were the Bocan's prisoners and will need rescuing themselves. I've sent a party to do this.'

'Good,' said Olive, who was looking much more like a fully qualified officer than a garden cadet. Nancy winked at her, but scowled at Toots. She had obviously not yet forgiven Toots for causing all this trouble. Toots shrank a little and hid behind Olive's arms.

'Now then,' said Nancy to her group of cadets. 'Half of you are to stay here with me and help the house fairies repair the dam, and the rest are to go with Olive. There are rather a lot of Bocans to see to, so you'd better get ready.'

The house fairies and river fairies set to work replacing the stones that had been chipped away and securing them with mud. A good deal of the dam had been dismantled and weakened, but the house fairies had only worked at quarter steam when the Bocans were forcing them and now that they were working to save the river instead of ruin it, they pulled out all the stops.

Toots, Olive and Nancy looked up when the black water above them began to bubble and churn. Hundreds of fish were all fighting to get to the surface.

'Oh wonderful! The fish have agreed to help us,' said Nancy. 'Just fill in all the holes,' she shouted with a wave and the teeming fish vanished beneath the surface. Nancy hurried over to the house fairies and joined in with a group who were cramming mud into the holes.

The fairy scout returned from the Bocan camp and saluted Olive.

'The Bocans are getting ready for war,' she reported. 'They know we're here and they're sharpening their swords and putting on their armour.'

'Thank you,' said Olive dismissing the scout. 'Well, Toots, you're always full of good ideas. What do you think we should do about the Bocans?'

Toots's eyes almost popped out of her head. Why was Olive asking her? She didn't have good ideas. All her ideas were stupid and they never worked. It had been her idea to steal the horn and flush the Naiad out to sea. Toots hung her head. Olive didn't really want to know what she thought.

Olive tapped Toots on the shoulder and bent close to her ear. 'I'm going to use one of your ideas anyway, even if you've forgotten you ever had it. Just watch.'

Toots looked puzzled.

'You'll see,' said Olive. 'Look at how fast the water is running through the sluice. With luck the rain will help us after all.'

Olive waved her arm and beckoned the twenty-seven river fairies to follow her as she flew with Toots towards the damp fires of the Bocan camp.

CHAPTER SEVENTEEN

~ A Chink in the Bocan Armour ~

Lightning flashed all about the flying fairies and the thunder roared. Toots wiped her wet face on her shoulder and scrunched up her eyes so that she wouldn't be blinded by the rain. Olive's flying goggles were spotted with raindrops and had steamed up on the inside.

Olive led the way. As she veered up into the reeds, the cadets followed.

Now the fairies flew in single file. It was hard flying, full of twists and turns to avoid colliding with the reeds, but Toots wasn't afraid. She knew that Olive was a very skilful flier even in terrible weather conditions and with an injured arm.

Soon they could see the Bocan tents through the haze of dirty smoke. Olive hovered and held up her arm and each fairy quickly and silently alighted on the nearest reed.

Quietly Olive briefed them on what to do at the

given signal and all of them nodded to show they understood. They sat there, eyes narrowed, peering up through the smoke, watching and waiting for the signal to attack.

In their camp the Bocans were busy with their armour. They needn't have bothered. The fairies had no weapons and couldn't do much except get out of the way if a Bocan raced towards them brandishing a sword or shooting arrows. The strangest thing was that the Bocans knew this. They knew that the fairies were no match for them, not really. But the Bocans had very strict dress codes when the time came for serious fighting and they were honour bound to adhere to them. A Bocan about to go into battle had to wear his heaviest armour and carry all his weapons so that he looked as ferocious as he possibly could.

As the lightning flashed Toots's eyes scanned the Bocan camp for Bladderwort. She wondered if he was still wearing her amethyst ring and if there would be any time for her to try and get it back. But she couldn't see the Bocan leader or her ring anywhere.

Soon all the Bocans were ready. Toots shivered at the sight of them and began to seriously doubt that she would ever go home again. The warriors looked terrifying as they clanked and stamped about in their armour, impatient to be off. Each Bocan carried at least five swords and two spears and four bows and fat quivers full of arrows. They gleamed splendidly as the raindrops settled like jewels on their shining chest plates and formidable helmets.

The female Bocans and the children were also armed and getting ready for battle. Their armour was nowhere near as splendid as the males', but it was still heavy and they all carried as many weapons as they possessed.

The Bocans were much more agile in the heavy armour than Toots had expected them to be and she could tell just from the way they were bending and stretching and practising with their swords that they would be quite adept at fighting despite all the added weight. A Bocan in full armour can only run at half normal speed but that is still twice as fast as most people.

Toots felt Olive bristle beside her on the next reed. The other fairies sat up too. Toots looked towards Bladderwort's tent.

Two Bocans pulled the curtained doors apart and after a moment Bladderwort, splendid in his golden armour and adorned with every glittering weapon from his hoard, waddled through. He had so many swords slung from his belt that he looked like a sword smith pedalling his wares and his back was quilled like a porcupine's with tall spears. His silver and gold helmet, which was dome-shaped with winged panels at the sides, sat low on his horrible head.

Bladderwort stopped and, turning his full body stiffly from left to right, solemnly surveyed his troops. Then with a slow careful nod of the heavy helmet, he pointed his arrow towards the dam and grunted. Toots saw her amethyst ring twinkling on his littlest finger.

But she didn't dare disturb Olive and ask her to help her to retrieve it. Toots knew that she had caused enough damage. She couldn't ask the fairies to help her again. She couldn't even whisper her wishes to Olive because the Bocans might hear her whispering. And that would give the game away. Toots looked at the amethyst twinkling in the light of the Bocan fire and closed her eyes. She knew that it was lost. She would never be able to get it back now.

Suddenly Bladderwort threw back his head and howled and his howl rang out above the thunder. The Bocans stampeded out of the camp, crashing through the reeds towards the place where the house and river fairies were desperately hurrying to repair the dam.

'Give them a moment to get clear of the camp,' hissed Olive, her eyes fixed on the backs of the marauding Bocans. 'Toots, do you remember when you wondered if the Bocans would get as angry as magpies if anyone tried to take their treasure away? That was what I meant when I said you'd given me a good idea. Now we're going to put it to the test. Let's hope they get good and angry!'

The last Bocans disappeared into the thicket of reeds.

'All right, everybody,' Olive shouted. 'Pick up as much of the Bocan hoard as you can carry and follow me.'

In a thick throng the river fairies left their reeds and flew swiftly into the deserted Bocan camp. They headed straight for the pile of Bocan treasure and hurriedly picked up the balls of silver foil, the broken chains, the bits of metal, the gold sweet wrappings and scraps of glitter and the other shiny things that the Bocans had purloined from various sources. Then, making as much noise as they possibly could, they flew after the Boscans into the reeds.

'Yip! Yip! Yip!' cried the river fairies. They flew with their feet pointing down to the ground, moving their legs to make them look as though they were running instead of flying.

A bocan knows instinctively when someone is interfering with his hard-earned treasure and it is the one thing he cannot bear. Though they had almost reached the fairies at the dam, each Bocan stopped dead in his tracks and, with a collective shriek of horror, turned as one and looked up at the fairies as they flew past.

'Get out of the way!' cried Olive as she flew past the house and river fairies who were repairing the dam. 'Bocans coming through!' The fairies scattered as the

Bocans burst on to the dam and charged after the treasure-bearing river fairies.

Bladderwort ran at their rear, his face twisted and terrifying in the electrifying light of the storm. He ran with two of his swords raised over his head and he roared like a wounded lion.

A hail of arrows whistled through the air, but they were knocked off target by the rain and they lost their strength. The fairies darted and dodged and avoided all of them.

'Hurry! Hurry!' cried Olive. She knew that another volley would not be far behind.

Bladderwort roared again. The Bocans were gaining on the fairies.

Toots clung to Olive's hands and closed her eyes. 'Please let Olive's plan work,' she whispered to herself. 'Please let it work.'

Then suddenly she could see the sluice only metres away along the dam.

The fairies zigzagged through the air to avoid the arrows and flew towards the sluice with their legs still running in the air. The Bocans treasure was heavy and the fairies were growing tired. The Bocans were gaining.

There was very little distance between the fairies and the Bocans now. The Bocans tore across the ground. Their armour and weapons clanked louder than the thunder. They were beside themselves with anger and their war cries were blood chilling and awful.

If the Bocans caught them now . . . Toots shuddered. She didn't want to think about that.

The fairies flew over the edge of the sluice and dropped the Bocan treasure. The Bocans in their anger didn't see the foaming waters. They only saw their treasure and the fairies running feet and took no notice of the ground beneath them until suddenly it was no longer there.

The first line of Bocan warriors could do nothing to stop themselves. Their screams rang out as they tumbled over the edge and plummeted into the raging waters. Those behind them were unlucky enough to see their fate and tried to stop, but were pushed over the edge by the Bocans at the rear who didn't know what lay in store and were all too eager to retrieve their treasure.

Bladderwort the Vain and Terrible was the only one who stopped in time. There were no Bocans left to trample him over the edge. He teetered on the brink of the sluice, the weight of his armour and weapons clanking back and forth would decide his fate. The fairies hovered in the rain and watched him. Bladderwort's armour creaked as he rocked and his horrid livid face was a mask of concentration. The fairies were fascinated. He was going to save himself by sheer determination.

Bladderwort teetered once more then settled back on his heels and took a step back on to safe ground. His revolting features erupted into a terrifying smile of triumph. He roared into the rain. He alone had foiled the fairies' plan. He raised his two swords high above his head and stamped angrily on the rain-soaked ground, but he had forgotten about the storm.

The bolt of lightning that at that moment split open the sky found a perfect conductor in Bladderwort's golden swords. It struck so fast that he didn't even have time to gasp. Bladderwort's armour fizzed with electricity and the swords fell from his hands.

'Olive!' cried Toots seizing the opportunity. 'Olive, he's wearing my ring!'

Olive flew swiftly to where Bladderwort stood at the edge of the sluice and hovered while Toots tried to retrieve her ring, but as she reached out towards him, his hand snapped shut. Even in death he could not bear to be parted from even the tiniest particle of his precious hoard.

His hand snapped shut so fast that the force of it reverberated through his body and he teetered forwards and tumbled over the edge into the foaming waters.

The river fairies would have cheered and congratulated Olive but they didn't have time. They had to hurry and help the others with the emergency repairs.

Toots stared up into the swirling waters as Olive flew past. There was no sign of Bladderwort. He had disappeared beneath the foam taking her mother's ring with him forever. Toots blinked up at the water. Olive patted her hand.

None of the river fairies even noticed the rain as they headed back to join their squadron. They knew that there was still a lot of work to do, but nothing could take away the fact that they had succeeded in getting rid of the Bocans.

CHAPTER EIGHTEEN

~ The Naiad Rising ~

When they reached the dam Toots looked up and was amazed to see how much of the repair work had already been completed. All the fairies were working as fast as they could and there was very little left to do. Captain May was pitching in and carrying two buckets full of clay to a group of house fairies on the north wall. Olive flew up beside her and quickly made her report.

'Very well done, Cadet Brown,' said the captain with a smile, then she bent her head and looked up at Toots. Toots felt very shy around the captain. She had been so wrong about her she didn't know where to put herself. She had to say something.

'Excuse me, ma'am,' she began quietly.

'Sorry,' barked the captain. She pointed down to the thunderous sky. 'You'll have to speak up.' The other fairies who were still hard at work pricked up their ears. Toots knew they were listening.

'I just wanted to say I was sorry,' Toots said in a louder voice as she held the silver-banded horn out to the captain.

'Oh!' said the captain pocketing the horn. 'Yes, I suppose you are. Now don't hang about. Lend a hand both of you. Hurry up. We'll be done with time to spare if there are no more interruptions.' She glanced up at the river which was getting steadily closer to the top of the dam. The water gushed through the sluice with a roar almost as loud as the thunder.

The storm was almost directly overhead and the thunder and lightning were less than three seconds apart. The lightning lit up the whole sky making a grey white ghost of the landscape as it flashed. Then the thunder roared.

Toots and Olive set to work carrying buckets of clay to the fairies, who were busily packing it into the spaces in the wall. Toots worked harder than she'd ever worked before. Her arms ached and so did Olive's, though to tell the truth it was Olive's wings that hurt the most, soaking wet and cold and tired with carrying almost twice their usual weight. But both Olive and Toots pushed their aches and pains away and concentrated on what they had to do.

In the back water the Naiad, tended by the frogs and toads and revived by the pouring rain, was recovering. She was a long way from her full strength, but she was so much better than she had been.

In less than half an hour Captain May flew over to Olive and asked to borrow her megaphone. Captain May put it to her lips.

'Listen up, everyone. I think that's enough. We're pretty certain that the dam will hold. You've all done very well, but I think it's time for us to help the house fairies home before they all collapse with exhaustion.'

She was cut off by the brilliant flash of lightning and the deafening crack of thunder. The storm was directly beneath them and it made the sky as bright as day.

The fairies screamed. In the eerie light of the storm they saw that the air below them was full of flying red beetles.

'Imps!' bellowed the captain through the megaphone. 'Battle stations, everyone!'

The beetles circled menacingly. They were gathering for their attack.

Toots clung to Olive as they flew with the other fairies to meet the beetles.

'Don't worry,' said Olive seeing that Toots was afraid. 'They look much worse than they are. We should be able to deal with them!' Toots wasn't sure that Olive was telling the truth. She remembered how strong Rebecca had been when she'd pulled her out of the Bocan tent. Perhaps Olive was just saying that to make her feel better.

The red beetles were huge and they had vicious mandibles that looked as if they could bite your head right off.

If the river fairies were afraid, they didn't show it. Even though most of them were exhausted after battling with the Bocans and rebuilding the dam, they flew down to meet the horrifying insect army with renewed energy.

The fairies had no weapons to fight the imps. They had no clever plans. They only had their fists and their feet, but they weren't afraid to use them. As a rule, fairies never fought unless they had to. Now they had to. They couldn't let the imps take over their river. The imps would destroy everything.

The river fairies launched themselves into the battle and soon discovered that one good kick on the left side of the underneath of a beetle would send them spinning off into the rain. Before long the air was full of spinning red beetles, their mandibles clashing on nothing as they flew out of control.

Toots started to think that Olive was right, the imps could be easily beaten. But they weren't beaten yet.

Suddenly the air was full of red flashes as the imps began to shift their shape. They stopped being beetles and became river fairies.

It took the river fairies a moment to see what was happening and in that moment the imps seized the advantage.

Soon the air was full of river fairies punching other river fairies. On the dam the captain could tell what was happening, but down in the air all was confusion.

Only an imp can tell an imp from a fairy instantly. Fairies can spot the difference if they can get a really good look at the impostors, but in the present situation they had no time for that.

It was a terrible shock to have someone you thought was on your side suddenly thump you. Now the river fairies began to lose the imps started to get the upper hand.

Toots looked back up at the river to see if there was any hope of help.

'Code Horse Retreat. Code Horse Retreat,' bellowed the captain through the megaphone.

Suddenly all the real river fairies in the air flew towards the river bank.

Olive dithered. 'My mind's gone blank,' she said in desperation. 'Toots, I know that that was in my exams, but I can't remember what Code Horse Retreat means.'

River fairies with menacing red sparks in their eyes surrounded Olive and Toots. Toots looked up. The captain had flown over to the weed-choked backwater. Toots saw the Naiad rising up.

'Think, Olive! Think!' she said as she kicked a river

fairy and hoped it was a imp.

Olive quickly recited a list of river plants, 'Water Arum no, Yellow Flag no, Ragged Robin! No, no, no.' Then she gasped. 'Of course. Horse! Mare's Tail. Quick, there's some over there where the others have gone.' Olive pointed to the tall bristly green fronds by the bank. 'Good job I didn't forget that in my exam!' she said as she broke away from the imps and raced after the other fairies.

'When you hear the captain give the signal,' Olive told Toots, 'Grab on to the nearest Mare's Tail and hold on for dear life.'

The imp fairies had followed the others and were trying to scratch and pinch them. The fairies fought them off. Toots and Olive flew up to where one river fairy was being tormented by a vicious fairy imp. Toots pulled the imp by the shoulder.

The imp spun round as the lightning flashed. It was Rebecca. 'Why hello, Toots,' it said smarmily, grinning in the rain. 'Are you being very brave now?'

Rebecca laughed at her.

The captain's voice boomed through the megaphone. 'All right, everyone. Code Horse now!'

Half the fighting fairies including Toots and Olive suddenly dived at the three tall fronds of mare's-tail and clung to them. The fairy imps who remained in the air were taken aback to see the fairies behave in this way.

They laughed at the fairies who were clinging to the plant as if their lives depended on it.

'Look,' whispered Olive. 'Look up there, beyond the imps. Look in the shallows now.'

Toots peered through the rain as the lightning flashed and saw an incredible sight. The Naiad was rising out of the shallows and as she did, the rain washed away the blanket weed from her head. Toots gasped. The Naiad was the most beautiful thing that she had ever seen. She was made entirely of water. A water spirit. Her hair was a cascading waterfall that tumbled over her shoulders and her face was made up of a swirling pattern of currents and eddies.

Toots forgot about the imps and the danger they posed. The sight of the water Naiad, the guardian of the river, rising up in all her clear watery loveliness, took her breath away. And she was struck with horror that she had ever thought the Naiad was dangerous or evil, that she had ever thought the Naiad was going to cause the destruction of the river. The Naiad *was* the river.

The imps were still laughing at the fairies who clung to the mare's-tail. Rebecca flew up to Toots and spitefully grabbed a handful of her hair. Toots winced in pain.

'Don't let go of the mare's-tail, Toots, whatever you

do,' whispered Olive. 'Hold really tight.'

More than anything Toots wanted to push Rebecca away. She wanted to get those horrid little claws out of her hair, but she knew she had to listen to Olive.

The Naiad turned towards the river bank and her lovely face grew stern. She pursed her beautiful mouth, puffed out the pools of her cheeks and blew.

The Naiad's breath created a fierce wind that sent the imps careening across the fields. Over and over they went like tumbling jacks far into the rainy night.

All the river fairies squealed as the mare's-tail to which they clung was blown flat against the bank. Toots hung on to it and gritted her teeth. She was in agony because Rebecca still held onto her hair. When the wind dropped and the mare's-tail sprang back up all the fairies squealed again.

The squealing stopped when they saw Rebecca. The fairies surrounded the mare's-tail where Rebecca still clung to Toots's hair.

Rebecca grinned at them sheepishly. She let go of Toots's hair and tried to pat it back in place. She didn't look so clever now that she was all alone and her friends had gone. She changed through several different disguises in rapid succession. She became Rebecca the fairy, then a Bocan, then a red beetle, then an imp again. The circle of fairies closed in on her.

Suddenly Rebecca squealed and pushed through the

circle. The fairies let her go and laughed as she blundered through the rain.

Toots looked over at the shallows and managed to catch the last sight of the river Naiad as she sank wearily back into the water.

'She won't be fully recovered yet,' said Olive sadly. 'And that effort may have cost her all her energy. Maybe tomorrow when she's stronger the fairies will be able to take her back upstream.'

CHAPTER NINETEEN

~ Robbie ~

The storm still raged as Olive, Toots and the rest of the river fairies flew back to the dam. When they arrived the captain quickly checked to see how they were and those who were not too badly bruised or injured after their fight with the imps were given orders to help carry the house fairies back to the cottages.

Toots and Olive helped in the evacuation and flew back and forth between the river and the cottages no fewer than five times.

Nancy was almost speaking to Toots when they'd finished because she'd seen how bravely Toots had fought the imps and how hard she'd worked on repairing the dam. If she'd known how sorry Toots felt about everything she would have spoken to her sooner.

As Nancy, Olive and Toots flew back to the cottages for the last time, Toots looked at the river overhead. She could see that it had risen a great deal, but she felt a surge of satisfaction when she saw that the dam looked solid and in no danger of collapsing. The water gushed through the sluice and Toots felt a pang when she thought of her ring which was now surely lost forever.

She turned away and tried not to think about what she'd say to her father when he found out. It was bad enough that she'd lost it; she didn't want to think about how angry her father would be as well.

It was wonderful to be out of the rain. The house fairies were thankful to be back in their own house and even though it was still rather a mess from the Bocan attack they were gracious hosts. Blankets were brought for everyone and mugs of hot cocoa were set on the table. It was almost worth battling Bocans and imps to end the day like this.

Toots sat on the window seat in the cottage's Upside Down House and looked out at the storm. She yawned and wondered what time it was.

Well, whatever time it was, she'd be able to go to sleep soon, she thought, and yawned again.

It was still raining, but the lightning now came a few seconds before the thunder which meant the storm was moving away. Toots pulled her blanket around her shoulders and held the mug of hot cocoa with both hands, blowing on it until it was cool enough to drink.

Olive sat down beside her. 'Well, that was quite an

adventure,' she said drying her hair on her blanket. 'I don't know how I'll explain where I've been when I get back to the garden. The C.O. here said she'll telephone my Group Captain to explain, but I think she'll have a job of it. It all sounds so far-fetched, don't you think?'

Toots smiled and imagined what her father and friends would think if she tried to explain where she'd been to them. Far-fetched wouldn't even begin to describe it.

'I'll take you home in a minute,' said Olive.

Toots nodded sleepily. That sounded good. She was ready to go home, ready to sleep. The lightning flashed outside the window. Toots looked up at the river beyond the trees and saw the island in the middle of the stream. The replenished river raged in torrents around it. Toots sat up and her cocoa slopped over the edges of her mug. She had seen something on the island in the rain and the wind, something that looked like a little animal shivering under the dripping bushes.

The thunder rolled over the fields and Toots waited, staring out at the blackness for the next flash of lightning. Then it came and lit up the island.

'Robbie!' she cried so loudly that the fairies in the room all stopped talking and turned towards her. 'Olive!' she said in a hoarse whisper. 'It's Robbie, out there on the island. Oh Olive, somebody's got to do something!'

Here was another thing that was all Toots's fault. She knew why Robbie was out there on that island. She remembered what Luke had said. Robbie had gone to meet the others at midnight. She should have told him they were only winding him up. She shouldn't have let them tease him.

Toots looked desperately at the fairies. What could they do? Even if they hadn't been worn out from their own battles, they were too small to be able to help. She would have to think of another way.

She put down her mug and threw the blanket off her shoulders and began to climb through the window onto the underside of the tree branch. She grabbed hold of Olive's arm. 'You've got to take me home right now. Please.'

Olive put down her mug and followed Toots out of the window. Toots ran along the tree branch and a second later Olive picked her up. Toots was so distressed that she didn't hear the fairies call goodbye to her.

Olive flew in through Toots's bedroom window and landed on the underside of the bed.

'Is there anything I can do?' she asked as she tied her rope around Toots's finger so that she could let her down to the floor gently.

Toots shook her head.

In less than a minute she was back to her own size and the right way up in her own world.

Without even untrying the rope on their finger. She wriggled out from under the bed and ran out of the room.

'Dad,' she cried, shaking her sleeping father roughly by the shoulder.

'Dad! Dad! Wake up. Robbie's in the river. Quick!'

CHAPTER TWENTY

~ Lucky Boy ~

Toots's father insisted that she had had a nightmare until she dragged him out of bed and made him look through the window. In the next flash of lightning he saw that she was telling the truth. Robbie really was on the island in the middle of the river.

All the blood drained out of her father's face. He grabbed a flashlight, pulled an anorak on over his pyjamas and hurried out of the door.

'Get to the phone box, call 999 and ask for an ambulance,' he shouted as Toots ran after him in the rain. 'He'll need a doctor. I'll meet you at Elaine's with Robbie.' Toots wanted to go with her father and check that Robbie was all right. She dithered on the path. Her father turned round in the rain and shouted, 'Toots, go to the phone!'

Later, as she sat in the living room of Elaine's cottage, she barely remembered calling the ambulance or hammering on Elaine's door. She could remember seeing her father wading through the rushing waters to where Robbie cowered beneath the brambles, and the red flashing lights of the ambulance when it arrived. And she could remember how frightened she'd been when she'd seen her father carrying Robbie wrapped in a blanket into the cottage.

Robbie's little face had been so pale that Toots had been afraid he was really very sick, but the ambulance men soon put her mind to rest. They'd told Elaine that Robbie would be fine. He just needed a good night's sleep and he'd be as right as rain.

'He's a very lucky little boy,' they'd said. 'Who knows how high the river might have climbed before the rain stopped? There might not have been an island by the end of the storm.'

Toots shuddered to think what might have happened then.

That night her father hugged her very hard before he tucked her up in bed. Toots was asleep before he'd finished saying the word 'goodnight'. Her father leaned over and closed the curtains. Toots hadn't even seen that the sky was growing light.

When Toots woke up it was already afternoon. She blinked out at the bright day. The storm had passed on and the sky was clear once more. She looked out of the window at the river where Luke and the others were playing on the rope swing.

She rubbed her finger. It felt as though there was something tried around it. Then she remembered Olive's cobweb rope and everything that had happened to her in the Upside Down World the night before.

'Olive!' she thought and she turned upside down and hung her head over the bed.

'Good afternoon,' said Olive cheerily through her megaphone. 'I was wondering when you were going to wake up.'

'Hang on, I'll come down.' Toots wriggled under the bed and Olive quickly brought her down to size. The pair of them sat on the edge of the bed swinging their legs and staring down at the bedroom ceiling.

'How's your friend Robbie?' asked Olive.

'I think he's going to be all right,' replied Toots, who didn't notice that for the first time she hadn't argued when someone called Robbie her friend.

'What did your Group Captain say when the C.O. telephoned her?'

Olive smiled a shy but very happy, secret sort of smile and blushed right to the tips of her hair.

'Well?' asked Toots who was dying to know that was going on.

'I think that Captain May must have spoken to my Group Captain and told her what happened.'

Olive paused. Toots couldn't stand it. 'Then what?'

Olive blushed and smiled again and her eyes crinkled up like two bright stars. 'Well, then my Group Captain said that because of the way I handled the emergency situation with the Bocans and the way I kept my cool under pressure and because my written exam results were good, that it doesn't matter that I missed the practical exam in the pond and I can graduate as a river fairy anyway.'

Olive smiled so much that her whole face radiated light.

'Oh, Olive,' cried Toots smiling. 'I'm so happy for you!' But then Toots stopped smiling. 'If you become a river fairy cadet, that means I won't be seeing you again, doesn't it?'

Olive looked surprised. Then she smiled and shook her head. 'Oh no, I see what you're thinking. You think I'll be half a day's drive away from your house. I won't be coming to this river. I've been offered a place at the river fairy cadet training centre in the stream at the bottom of your road. I won't be very far away at all. Only two houses.'

'Oh, Olive,' said Toots who now really couldn't have been more pleased for her friend. 'Congratulations!'

'I brought your bucket back,' said Olive with another smile. 'You left it when you hurried off last night.' Toots took the bucket and hugged it to her middle.

'I'm so sorry I messed things up,' she said quietly. 'I'm sorry that I took the horn and I'm sorry that I lost the instruction book. What will the captain do now when she wants to change the weather? How will she know what to do?'

'Don't worry,' replied Olive. 'The captain knows those instructions by heart. So do most river fairies if they're worth their salt. Even I know one or two of those tunes. They were part of my exams.'

Toots's eyes opened wide. 'But, Olive, why didn't you or the captain or somebody stop the storm?'

Olive shook her head. 'It wasn't possible. Once a storm has been summoned you can't just stop it. That would cause all kinds of havoc. It's not like trying on a pair of shoes, you know. Sometimes you just have to take what comes and deal with it. I think everyone dealt with the storm pretty well. Don't you?'

Toots didn't say anything. She didn't think she'd dealt with anything very well at all. Olive nudged her.

'When they knew I was coming to see you all the house and river fairies wanted me to say goodbye to you for them.'

'Oh,' said Toots remembering all the blunders she'd made and blushing. Perhaps they didn't think she was so awful after all. 'Say goodbye to them from me as well, will you?' She stared down at the ceiling and after a moment asked, 'Olive, no one happened to find my ring, did they?'

Olive shook her head. 'I'm afraid not. There was so much work to do this morning tidying up the Upside Down House and doing proper repairs on the dam and finding a way to bring the Naiad upstream to safety that I doubt if anyone had time to search for your ring.'

'Oh,' said Toots. Olive patted her hand.

'Tell you what,' she said with a bright twinkle in her eye. 'I'll do my best to hunt it down and get it back to you somehow. Just keep your eyes open,' she added, the twinkle brightening. 'It will probably turn up when you least expect it.'

'Thanks,' said Toots. 'I'd better go. I want to see Robbie and find out how he is.' Toots lowered her chin and pulled a face. 'I want to try and be nice to Robbie today. I've promised myself I'll play with him and do whatever he wants to do no matter how stupid and boring it seems.'

'It might not be that bad,' said Olive. 'You might even enjoy yourself.' Toots shrugged. Olive smiled. 'Oh, one last thing. As soon as you get back, will you open your ring box and leave it open so that I can travel home in it when the time comes?'

Toots said she would.

Then Olive sent her back to the right side up world and, while Toots could still remember that there was an

Upside Down World at all, she opened her ring box, put the tiny bucket that she could feel against the palm of her hand inside, and set the box open just under the bed.

CHAPTER TWENTY-ONE

~ Not Such a Stupid Game ~

Toots found Robbie sitting on the river bank just downstream of the dam. He was scraping at the ground with a stick. He looked up and squinted at her as she approached, but he didn't say anything.

'Hello,' she said crouching beside him and feeling a little awkward. 'How are you feeling?'

'Okay,' he replied, looking back down at the stick as though it was much more interesting to look at than Toots. The other children were playing upstream by the island. Chasing each other around and screaming a lot. It looked like fun, but Toots had promised herself that she would play with Robbie and not leave him out anymore.

'What are you doing?' she asked, sitting down beside him.

'Nothing,' he replied.

'Do you want to play hide and seek or tag or . . .?'

'No.' Robbie stood up and walked a little way away from her.

Toots stared into the river. It promised to be a very dull afternoon. Robbie wasn't even going to make one of his stupid suggestions, or offer to tell her about minerals or stones or anything. Toots wracked her brains to try and think of what would make him see that she wasn't just trying to tease him or wind him up. Perhaps if she showed some interest in something he liked. She tried to remember some of the ideas he'd plagued her with in the past.

'We could pan for gold if you like,' she said, remembering Robbie's suggestion that everyone else had ignored. Robbie's shoulders rose a millimetre. 'That's if you really know how to do it,' Toots added.

Robbie stood with his hands on his hips. Toots looked sideways at him. She could tell he was trying to decide whether to trust her or not. He threw his stick into the stream.

'All right,' he said. 'I'll show you.'

Never in a hundred years would Toots have thought that playing one of Robbie's games could have been fun, but to her surprise she thoroughly enjoyed herself that afternoon. Her dad had been right. Robbie was quite interesting when you really listened to what he had to say.

The afternoon whizzed by. Robbie showed her how to sieve through the silt that they brought up from the bottom of the stream and he told her the names of the different types of rocks and pebbles they found.

The sun was just setting when Toots's dad appeared through the trees and called them into supper. 'Two minutes,' he said as he headed back to the cottage.

Toots started to climb up the bank, but just as she got to the top Robbie called to her.

'Hey, look at this,' he said swirling the water through the sieve. Something glinted gold against the mesh. Toots narrowed her eyes and took a step towards him. Robbie dipped the sieve in the water again to rinse what he'd found.

'I told you we'd find some treasure,' said Robbie lifting it out again.

Toots peered in. It wasn't gold. It was just rubbish that had collected in the sieve. Bits of old gold and silver sweet wrappers and scraps of wire and metal. It wasn't really treasure at all. But then as she looked at the little pile her heart stopped.

There was treasure there after all. She sifted through the sweet wrappers and her heart leaped as her fingers closed upon the unmistakable shape of her amethyst ring. Toots picked it out and rinsed it in the stream.

'It's my ring,' she gasped as she held it high above her head. The purple stone glinted in the light of the setting sun.

Toots had no idea how it had ended up in the river.

Her memories of the river fairies and the Bocans and the marsh imps were now nothing more than a dusty dream. Toots shook her head. She didn't remember Olive telling her that she would try and find the ring for her. She didn't even remember that she'd ever known anyone called Olive. She hadn't the faintest idea how she'd lost her ring in the first place, but she never forgot that if it hadn't have been for Robbie and his not so stupid game, she would never have found it again.

Toots slipped the ring on her fattest finger. It was just ever so slightly too big.

'Toots! Robbie! Supper!' called her father through the trees.

'Come on.' Toots grabbed Robbie's hand and pulled him to his feet. 'I'll race you to the table. Last one there's a sissy,' she cried as she leapt up the bank and ran through the trees.

192